ORIGINATION

ORIGINATION

Twelve Tales of Inner Mind and Outer Matter

S.L. Leitner

All stories and characters in this book are fictitious. Any similarity to actual persons, living or dead, is coincidental.

Copyright © 2025 S.L. Leitner. Visit S.L. Leitner's website at www.sleitnerbooks.com.

All rights reserved.

No portion of this book may be reproduced, distributed, or transmitted in any form or by any means, including photocopying, recording, or other electronic or mechanical methods, without prior written permission from the author, except as permitted by U.S. copyright law. For permission requests, contact info@sleitnerbooks.com.

Book cover art and book design by Christy Levine.

First paperback and ebook edition: November 2025.

Paperback ISBN: 979-8-9917198-0-3

EBook ISBN: 979-8-9917198-1-0

To my daughter Christy, who created the book's beautiful cover art and designed its interior.

To Doug Purcell, who inspired me to commit to getting back to writing fiction and to publish.

To Steve Sarette, Ali Ahsan, Johnny Klonaris, Phil Kwan, James Wilson, and Rich Pellicone, who read these stories without suffering adverse consequences. Mostly without suffering from adverse consequences.

To all those who put up with me while engaging in this journey, especially my daughter and her cats, Natsu and Ivy, who made up for constantly shedding all over everything by being incredibly cute and available for scritches.

Table of Contents

Introductory Blather 11
One Thing Leads to Another 13
    Showtime at the Apocalypse Theater 15
    Achoo! 23
Weird Scenes Inside the Neighborhood 37
    Davi 39
    Secret Agent Emily 45
    Creating a Masterpiece 55
    Blanque's Suburbia 63
    Scrimshaw Jones 71
Life During Collegetime 101
    Every Mad Dog Has His Day 103
    The Great Cafeteria Food Fight and Ice Cream Raid of 1981 109
What I Talk About When I Talk About God 121
    The Irate Businessman 123
    I Am 147
    The Gardener 153

- Behind the Scenes 163
  - Behind the Scenes of *Showtime at the Apocalypse Theater* 165
  - Behind the Scenes of *Achoo!* 167
  - Behind the Scenes of *Davi* 169
  - Behind the Scenes of *Secret Agent Emily* 171
  - Behind the Scenes of *Creating a Masterpiece* 173
  - Behind the Scenes of *Blanque's Suburbia* 175
  - Behind the Scenes of *Scrimshaw Jones* 177
  - Behind the Scenes of *Every Mad Dog Has His Day* 179
  - Behind the Scenes of *The Great Cafeteria Food Fight and Ice Cream Raid of 1981* 181
  - Behind the Scenes of *The Irate Businessman* 182
  - Behind the Scenes of *I Am* 183
  - Behind the Scenes of *The Gardener* 185
- About the Cover Illustration and Title 189
- About the Author 193

S.L. LEITNER

Introductory Blather

Fiction is truth shrouded in lies.
—S.L. Leitner

I aim to weave entertaining stories. I don't write in a particular genre because ideas ricochet off everything, everywhere, and they lead to everywhere and everything. Rod Serling could introduce some of these stories; others could only be introduced by a clown.

In this circus of short stories, you'll meet a little old lady on a spy mission, a rambunctious group of children, a perfectionist artist, God (three times), and a Mad Dog, among others. I culled these odd bookfellows from a period of time ranging from college to COVID and beyond.

Because I'm a bit genre-agnostic, I split the book into four themed sections. And because I can't help playing with words, each section has its own introduction and a few words on the theme.

Fun fact: several of these stories are based on real-world events. Maybe even more than some, for all I know.

Soon after I finished writing the short story *Achoo!*, I met a guy named Doug Purcell. We were both working as technical writers at a network security company. It turned out that Doug had self-published five books (you can find them all on Amazon), including a handy book on self-publishing. Talking about writing and publishing with Doug kindled (Kindled?) my desire to perpetrate my stories on the unsuspecting, and possibly—but not likely—innocent public.

For each story, there's a corresponding look *Behind the Scenes* that reflects on some aspect of the story or its genesis. If that's not interesting to you, skip it. I promise it won't be on the test.

In fact, there won't even be a test.

So much for having this book taught in schools.

Visit S.L. Leitner's website at www.sleitnerbooks.com.

S.L. LEITNER

One Thing Leads to Another

One thing leads to another
You told me something wrong, I know I listen too long but then
One thing leads to another, yeah, yeah, yeah
    —The Fixx, One Thing Leads to Another

Sometimes, one seemingly inconsequential action leads to much larger, seemingly unrelated actions, like the chaos theory staple of a butterfly flapping its wings and then halfway around the world, the flapping wings somehow cause an earthquake or a tsunami. These stories are about such seemingly inconsequential actions and what they led to.

- *Showtime at the Apocalypse Theater*
  Gretelhans Blöderschmidt invades Switzerland to avenge aggrieved Liechtensteiners everywhere.
- *Achoo!*
  The Junior College of American Pathology has a problem.

S.L. LEITNER

Showtime at the Apocalypse Theater

Once again, it's showtime at the Apocalypse Theater, and I am as eager as ever to play the charming and sagacious host of *Our Favorite History*, or at least, that's what I call the show. Twittering, buzzing, squealing sounds of youthful life flood the cavern. I stand for a moment, eyes closed, the flood washing over me, soaking into the deepest creases of my skin. I open my eyes and raise my right hand, palm out, as far as arthritis allows.

I miss prescription pain killers.

Silence mists over us, extinguishing chatter in the same way a slowly drawn curtain gradually extinguishes sunlight flooding into a room. When all I can hear is children trying not to make a sound, I begin.

"Nobody ever quite believes how it started. Everybody thought it would begin somewhere in the Middle East or maybe in Taiwan. Kind of appropriate if it would have been the Middle East; the end of civilization starting in its cradle." I can't help a corner of my mouth from curling upward as I continue, "But you don't want to hear that story again."

"Yes we do! Tell us again how the world ended!" clamor all the children in shrill unison. "Pleeeeeeese!"

"We-ell," I stretch my words and put on my most doubtful face, "I don't know."

The leader of the children stands before me, makes her eyes real big, on-the-verge-of-tears starry, and pleads, "C'mon, Historian. We want to hear it."

Her lovely face holds just the right hints of disappointment and longing, holds them in cold and calculated study, yet it affects me. I clutch the smooth knob of my walking stick with both hands, drawing from it strength with which I have endowed it over the years; every crutch takes at least as much as it gives. "Seems like I just told that story yesterday," I say.

"Tell us, tell us!" they shout as they all jump up and wave their arms. I can almost feel their motion in the air. The leader asks, "What do you want from us, Historian?"

"Vicodin would be nice, but I'd gratefully take plain aspirin." I hurry on before the girl can question what those things were. "But since I won't get them, I'll settle for just your smiles and a few moments of your attention, my dear."

I know it doesn't sound like much for payment, but it's a taste of life when everything else is dead, a taste of joy when everything else is pain. These children are my hope and my sanity when every other snapshot of the future is hopeless and insane.

I sit on the most comfortable rock in the cave and watch the children settle into a crescent at my feet, jostling one another for the closest spots. The high-pitched yips and giggles fade into expectation.

"The first day of the end of the world came thirty years ago, when a tiny country called Switzerland began handing out speeding tickets to citizens of an even tinier country called Liechtenstein. Now both of these nations between them could fit into your pocket with room left over for Luxembourg." I pause a moment, even though I know none of the children will so much as snicker.

"Liechtenstein complained that the speed limit suddenly dropped when you crossed the border into Switzerland, which often happened on journeys that took folks farther than next door, and that the change wasn't marked in their direction. The Swiss read the message, had a good laugh, and then with typical Helvetian tidiness, they tossed it in the recycling bin and went back to making clocks and chocolate and army knives and so forth.

"Naturally, the government of Liechtenstein was outraged over this insult. In protest, they sent the smelliest piece of their smelly Liechtenberger cheese to the Swiss heads of state."

"How could a smelly cheese protest?" asks an older boy.

"Well," I reply, "they wanted to show the Swiss they meant business. The chosen cheese had been kept in a dark, moist closet for more than ten years, basking in its own fetid stench, until the smell itself had grown a long, moldy green beard that reached out and tickled the inside of your nose."

"Eeeeuwww!" shrills a child near the back of the gathering.

"Eeeeuwww is right!" I agree with a hearty nod. "And the Swiss agreed too, because they took this as a strong protest indeed. But once mixed with crackers and a bit of wine the protest was soon over, and the Swiss gave their neighbors speeding tickets at an accelerated rate—so to speak." My gaze sweeps across the room and I chuckle, not so much at my poor joke as at the children's faces, screwed up in various contortions of incomprehension as they try to figure out what I think is funny.

"This eating of the smelly cheese absolutely infuriated the government of Liechtenstein. Liechtenstein's prince decided to take immediate military action. He amassed his troop on the border and issued an impassioned challenge to the Swiss to do battle."

I lean forward, my weight propped up by the strength of my walking stick, and beckon the children closer, inviting them to join the conspiracy of my tale. "Now, the Swiss outnumbered their tinier neighbors a hundred to one, and they had been prepared for an invasion since way back in the late 1930s because of Hitler and the Nazis. So the Swiss had another good laugh, and then scrambled up into the Alps to find all the hidden caches of weapons left over from World War Two. The Swiss had supposedly remained neutral for more than 300 years at that point, but for once, a war had come up that they were certain they were going to win!" I laugh, and this time the children laugh with me.

"The Swiss scrambled from peak to peak, digging through glaciers and burrowing under snow banks, following old maps the dog had chewed up, valiantly searching for the rifles, handguns, machine guns, grenades, and ammunition hidden on every peak of the Alps. Problem was, nobody could find anything. Either the maps were wrong, or they'd been used to line bird cages, or the landmarks had simply changed over the years. But the Swiss were a determined people.

"Now in the meantime, while the Swiss were out of town schussing all over the Alps—"

"What's schussing?" asks a short-haired little darling in the front row.

"It's skiing, dear. Now shush! As I said, while the Swiss were out of town schussing all over the Alps, Liechtenstein hardly remained idle. The troop massed on the border snuck across, sticking carefully to the speed limit to avoid getting a ticket. When the troop arrived in the capital city of Bern, he found it deserted. Even the—"

"Don't you mean they?" a boy calls from the back.

"No, I mean he," I explain patiently. "Liechtenstein's troop consisted of one young man named Gretelhans Blöderschmidt. Now when Gretelhans Blöderschmidt arrived in the capital city of Bern, even the shopkeepers were in the Alps, busy looking for the arms caches. So Gretelhans walked along the promenade above the icy Aare river, admiring the view of Switzerland's famous Eiger, Mönch, and Jungfrau mountains, which were alive with Swiss frantically searching for arms. Then he came upon the building the government occupied when it wasn't on fact-finding missions to the Bahamas or looking for World War Two artifacts.

"Well, the troop was surprised to find the place unguarded. He consulted with his commanding officer, who also happened to be Gretelhans Blöderschmidt, and then walked in and claimed the foyer, the building, the capital, and the whole country for Liechtenstein. Feeling a bit tuckered out from the day's work, Gretelhans took a futile smell around for leftovers from Liechtenstein's cheese, then settled down to the business of government and took a nap.

ORIGINATION

"Now that afternoon, the cleaning lady showed up and got a nasty shock when she found the flag of Liechtenstein propped up in an umbrella stand in the doorway. She ran outside screaming, in a dignified *Swiss* way of course. Before poor Gretelhans knew what had happened, a horde of outraged Swiss had surrounded him, their army knives unfolded in a confusing medley of useful implements. Some threatened to uncork him, some brandished can openers, while others viciously threatened to trim his fingernails too close. Outnumbered and armed only with his car keys and a radar detector, Gretelhans was forced to surrender."

One of the girls gasps. "What did the Swiss do to him, Historian?"

I smile benignly at the child. "Well, I'll tell you. The very next day, the Swiss renewed their demands for Liechtenstein to pay the speeding tickets. To show their seriousness, the Swiss cut off one key from the troop's keychain, sent it with the message, and threatened to send one key every day until Liechtenstein relented. Within a week, all the keys had been ruthlessly removed from the keychain, but Liechtenstein stood fast and refused to pay the tickets."

"Did it really hurt Gretelhans when they cut off his keys?" asks the youngest boy, his eyes so wide they seem on the verge of meeting on the other side of his head.

"Well, he was very fond of those keys." I lower my head a moment to hide my grin before telling him, "They belonged to the only car in Liechtenstein that hadn't been impounded for nonpayment of speeding tickets. You see, to get back at the Swiss, Liechtenstein had lowered the speed limit coming from Switzerland into Liechtenstein. The problem was that the Swiss never went to Liechtenstein, so the speed trap only caught Liechtensteiners returning home.

"Anyway, the Swiss didn't know what to do to get Liechtenstein to pay up. They tried dismantling the radar detector and sending it back one component at a time, but in spite of the fact that it was their only radar detector, Liechtenstein remained unmoved. They even thumbed their noses at the Swiss by putting the radar detector back together. Switzerland tried political pressure, economic pressure, and decreasing the tire pressure on Liechtenstein's remaining unimpounded vehicle, but nothing worked.

"Finally, in a fit of pique, the President of the Swiss Confederation fired off a nuclear bomb he'd been saving for the first of August Confederation Day parade and flattened the Prince of Liechtenstein's royal palace. When the other nuclear powers found out Switzerland had used its bomb, they all had to try out theirs, too." I glance down at the darkness of the cold rock floor between the folds of my robe; my parched lips press together.

"Well, the rest is history. Soon there wasn't anything left but a few pockets of people, and most of those were wiped out by radiation carried on the winds. Only those who took to the deepest caves lived, and only those who stay in the caves still do."

Eventually, I look up again. "And that, my children, is how the world ended."

They all stare at me, as if expecting more, even though they know the story is over. All their pretty faces, all their ocean eyes and dark pupils flecked with sparkles of reflected light, like so many beautifully flawed pearls. And they wonder why tears spill silently from my eyes after this absurd story, this fitting end to an absurd improbability.

I lean heavily on my walking stick and push myself to my feet, my knees cracking in protest. I marvel at the children's eternal youth and innocence, their mischievous loveliness. These children, they do keep me alive somehow, hoping somehow.

But that's enough for one day. I don't have much energy, and I must conserve what little I have if I am to live. Energy is life, life is energy, and both of mine are limited. The precious clamor of children's voices rises in the aftermath of the tale as I shuffle to the back of the cave. I wonder which tale I will tell them tomorrow night.

Because pain is also part of life, I look over my shoulder as I flip the simulator switch off. The children vanish as if they had never existed, leaving behind only the glimmer of hope that they really do exist somewhere.

ORIGINATION

S.L. LEITNER

Achoo!

"Damn hay fever," Jackson thought. He checked his gloves and hoped to hell he wouldn't sneeze into the biohazard suit's faceplate, both for the sake of his vision and the endless jokes he'd suffer at the hands of his co-workers. He didn't want to be known as Snotface Jackson.

He entered the storage room through the bio-lock. As he waited for the air to cycle, Jackson tried not to think about the yellow coat of seasonal pollen shellacking every outdoor surface. That was his first mistake.

He looked for the drawer labeled "Inert", found it, and then made his second mistake. He tried to stem the tide of the tsunami sneeze his brain had planted in his sinuses by "not thinking" about pollen, as if it were possible not to think of something you had already thought of.

Then Jackson made his third mistake by doggedly reaching for the handle of the drawer. The tsunami crash-landed with a spasmodic "Achoo!" just before his hand reached the handle. Eyes slitted and watery from the sneeze, he grasped the handle and pulled the drawer completely out of the large cabinet. The drawer was a rectangular box with a handle, covered on top. It contained two large, sealed trays of vials, each of which required a key to open. Jackson shook his head and unleashed the predictable follow-up sneeze as he turned toward the bio-lock exit, holding the drawer with both hands. The sneezes hadn't felt too wet, Jackson reflected; maybe nobody would notice a little spray on the windshield…

"That finishes number three of five samples," he told himself as he opened the top of the box. He placed each locked tray into a machine that would unlock it, remove the vials from the tray, and then add them to the Influenza Test Kits. The Junior College of American Pathology would then send the kits to their partner labs in the United States and around the world for research.

Jackson looked up as a coworker walked in. "Hey, Tenorio," he greeted her.

She grinned and shook her head. "Did you just dive into a swamp head first, Snotface?"

⧖   ⧖   ⧖   ⧖   ⧖

The Junior College of American Pathology is essentially a minor league system for the College of American Pathology, which is responsible for testing and analyzing pathogens to prevent the spread of and find cures for potentially threatening pathogens. Promotion to the College of American Pathology occurs when an expert panel determines that a Junior College member has become pathological enough to join the big league.

The Junior College had been trusted with the latest influenza test kit composition and distribution mainly because it was a fairly routine job and the big league players were tired of doing work they perceived as menial. The Junior College of American Pathology's Director of Proficiency Testing led the program and introduced many innovations, including saving a ton of cash by outsourcing the test kit packaging operation. The cost-cutting move won enthusiastic approval from the College's board.

Dr. Andrew Rigby, Deputy Director of Proficiency Testing at the Junior College of American Pathology, had paid his dues by being a faithful minion of the Junior College's Director of Proficiency Testing. Dr. Rigby was on the cusp of acceptance to the full College, so close to being deemed pathological enough that in his mind's eye, he had already laid out and decorated his new office. And then *this* had happened, no fly in the

ORIGINATION

ointment but a full-grown elephant.

The Junior College Director of Proficiency Testing had resigned, very unexpectedly as far as Dr. Rigby was concerned, at least until he was informed about what had happened. The last anyone heard, the director was running from his office muttering something about "unexplored areas of the Amazon."

And now Dr. Andrew Rigby sat outside the office of the Director of Proficiency Testing, the real one for the College of American Pathology, not just the Junior College. The admin told Dr. Rigby he could go in now. Dr. Rigby found "could" to be rather darkly funny because he didn't think there was an actual choice.

Dr. Rigby grasped the arms of the chair he had waited in, drew a deep breath, stood up, and then walked stiffly into the office. The Director looked at Dr. Rigby and waited, neither blinking nor looking away. Dr. Rigby found himself studying the polished black tips of his rubber-soled lab shoes, losing himself in the crinkled creases behind his toes where the shoes flexed when he walked. He wanted to dive into those creases and escape in the labyrinth of wrinkled leather, but The Director had other ideas.

"Come on Dr. Rigby, you said this was important." She folded her hands on the mahogany desktop. "I do have other duties."

"I said it was urgent," Dr. Rigby corrected without looking up.

"Urgent, but not important?"

"Urgent and important," Dr. Rigby admitted, still not looking up. "And rather a lot of both."

The Director sighed. "Either your shoes are fascinating or you're trying to tell me something I really don't want to hear."

It was Dr. Rigby's turn to sigh. Deeply. "Uh, you know those influenza proficiency test kits we sent to labs all around the world?"

"I seem to recall something about that. Hundreds of labs involved, wasn't it?"

"Thousands," Dr. Rigby said, nodding. "A lot of university labs get them—they're safe for student experiments because the samples are always inert." Then he corrected himself. "Er, almost always inert."

"I'm not going to like what you're about to tell me, am I?"

"Um, no," Dr. Rigby agreed. "Probably not."

"Get on with it," said The Director. "When the medicine tastes bad, it's best to take it down in one quick shot."

"Yes."

"Yes," The Director agreed.

Silence.

"*Now*, Dr. Rigby."

"Yes. Ahem. You see, one of the cost-cutting moves the former JC Director made was to use a third party to fill the sample vials, store and pack the samples, and send them to our partner labs, not just for this test kit, but for all samples and test kits. You know, bulk savings. When they packed the vials for the Influenza Proficiency Test Kit shipment, it was supposed to contain only dead virus samples, but apparently something happened and they put in the wrong vial for one of the samples." Dr. Rigby continued to discover new capillaries of wrinkles in his leather shoes. "The vial has a particularly virulent active influenza sample."

The Director leaned in. "Just how virulent?"

Dr. Rigby kept his head down, trying to hide how miserable he felt. "Extremely virulent," he squeaked. "And communicable. Extremely communicable."

"Is it deadly?"

"If you die from it, yes. If you survive, then not really."

"That was very helpful. Let me try again: What's the mortality rate?"

"We're not sure. This virus hasn't been seen in a long, long time, but we think that with the proper precautions, it wouldn't be as bad as, say, the Black Plague, although maybe worse than the Spanish Flu epidemic. It is a bit of a super-flu."

"A super-flu? Great. And this went out to thousands of labs?"

Dr. Rigby shook his head vigorously. "Oh no. We think only about five hundred went out and that's less than ten percent of the test kits."

"So at least you know who has the active samples?"

"Well…not exactly. We don't know which of the five thousand, one hundred and twenty-seven test kits we sent to our partner labs had the active sample and which test kits had the harmless, inactive sample."

The Director's eyes narrowed. "Do you at least know who received the test kits?"

"Oh, yes, Ma'am. The former JC Director contracted with FedShip.

ORIGINATION

They're very good about keeping a paper trail and confirming their deliveries, so we know exactly which labs received kits. We were a bit surprised that they'd ship dangerous biohazardous material, but they said they ship dangerous biohazardous material right alongside the other packages—only more carefully."

The Director's face completed a fade to granite gray on a stormy day. The thought surfaced that she was long overdue for a vacation. Perhaps to a very remote area. The unexplored portion of the Amazon might not be a bad idea. "And what do you suggest to do about this, Dr. Rigby?"

"Ah, me? I wasn't really involved with the project and I'm only the Deputy Director at the JC level."

"Since the Director at the JC level is no longer with us, you're the new Director at the JC level, Dr. Rigby."

"Oh." Dr. Rigby couldn't think of anything else to say.

"Congratulations. Now what are you going to do about this?"

"But…but I thought with the way things are, maybe a…more senior person would take over this crisis—maybe your Deputy Director?"

"The Deputy Director is…unavailable at this time," The Director replied, realizing that the timing of the Deputy Director's sudden decision yesterday to pursue her "lifelong dream—an Etsy shop for macramé designs" may have been slightly more than coincidental. "You're more familiar with the situation, anyway, Dr. Rigby." Her sour expression magically crossed the room and found a home on Dr. Rigby's face. "And it can't be me, I'm about to go on a long-planned vacation that I've delayed twice already. You're it."

"Oh." Dr. Rigby still couldn't think of anything else to say. *You're it.* As if they were playing tag to see whose career was going to crash and burn and now he was the only one playing the game.

"So I repeat: what are you going to do?"

"Well, uh, we could…no, no, that won't work…or…no, no." He began to pace the room as great thinkers do. And as not-so-great thinkers do. "Well…the labs that received the test kits are our partners. Couldn't we just ask them to destroy the vial and we'll send them an inert version to replace it?" He rubbed his hands. "After all, they are our partners." Dr. Rigby's voice steadied. "I'm sure they'll be happy to cooperate, sure. I mean, what else can we do?" He tried to laugh but it came out more like a bray. "It's not like we're Mission Impossible and we have mini explosives in each vial so we can detonate them from here, right?" He glanced up and asked, "Do we?" before staring back down at his shoes.

The Director stood up. "Mission Impossible. Christ, where do they come from? Fine then. Your mission, Dr. Rigby, and you're damn well going to accept it, is to persuade all of our partners to destroy those vials. By yesterday."

Dr. Rigby wiped his brow and felt the dampness through his sleeve. "I guess, yes, well, at least most of the labs are in the United States, OK."

"That's good. How many are not in the United States?"

"Only one hundred and seven."

"Only?"

"Considering that more than five thousand labs received samples, that's a pretty small percentage."

"And where are those labs, Dr. Rigby?"

"Oh, they're all our trusted research partners," Dr. Rigby said brightly, divesting his attention from his shoes.

"That doesn't sound too bad," said The Director. "Who are our trusted research partners?"

"Countries like Switzerland, Canada, Japan, Germany, India, Australia, and France. In fact, it was a lab in Canada that alerted us to the issue."

"Well that doesn't sound too bad, except for France."

"And Lebanon, Ukraine, Chad, and a few others," muttered Dr. Rigby. "Seventeen more countries in total."

"Dr. Rigby." It sounded like the start of reading a prison sentence. "You will contact those foreign partners and you will convince them to destroy those vials. And you will do it *quietly*. Very, very quietly." The Director walked around her desk and held Dr. Rigby's unwilling but frozen gaze. "Can you imagine what would happen if news of this got out? We would be laughingstocks. We would never be trusted again." She took a step closer. Dr. Rigby wanted to take a step back but his legs wouldn't cooperate. The Director shouted, "*The CDC would get all our grant money!*"

"A lot of people might die too," said Dr. Rigby and instantly regretted it.

"*Your career would be over!*"

Dr. Rigby cowered and then recovered slightly. "But…but I wasn't in charge!"

ORIGINATION

"You are now." The Director went back to her chair and sat. "Get results, get them fast, get them quietly, or it'll be your name in the headlines when the epidemic hits. Now go."

⌛ ⌛ ⌛ ⌛ ⌛

At some level, Dr. Rigby realized that the MyPhonio™ Voice-over-IP phone interface staring back at him from his monitor wouldn't make the calls itself. His new Deputy Director sat across the desk, ready to provide moral support but no more eager to start than Dr. Rigby.

Dr. Rigby knew he had to start calling and dive into the pain instead of prolonging the agonizing anticipation of the pain. May as well begin with the Swiss and try to get off to a good start. If there was anyone you could count on after the Canadians, it had to be the Swiss. He mumbled, "MyPhonio, call our partner lab in Basel." His phone dutifully performed the database lookup and initiated the call.

On the third ring, someone answered and said, "Hier Herr Doktor Knutter."

"Hello Hair Dock-tor KaNewter, it's Dr. Rigby, Deputy Director—I mean Director—of the Junior College of American Pathology. We recently sent you the Influenza Proficiency Test Kit and also a really important alert about an active virus that was inadvertently placed in the kit. Did you receive the alert?"

"Ah, Dr. Rigby, ja, we received the request from your office." Herr Doktor Knutter glanced at a fidgety white-coated younger man sitting across the desk from him in his office. "And, ja, we destroyed the vial."

"All the super-flu is destroyed?"

"We destroyed the vial you sent us," Knutter confirmed. "We videotaped the destruction and will send it to you for your records."

Dr. Rigby muted the phone and whispered to his new Deputy Director, "Well, at least that's one we know for sure has been destroyed." He smiled and unmuted the phone. "Thank you, Hair Dock-tor KaNewter, we appreciate your cooperation. Have a good evening."

"And you also." Knutter hung up and turned to the fidgeting man.

"Well?"

"Herr Doktor Knutter," the younger man said, "I am not comfortable with this. We are not telling the Americans the truth."

"We are telling the Americans exactly the truth," replied Knutter. "I told them we destroyed the vial. And we did destroy the vial, the records prove it."

"But the super-flu virus was no longer in that vial when we destroyed it," the younger man complained.

"This should not concern you, Herr Doktor," replied Knutter with an edge of annoyance. "After all, who better to control such a weapon than a completely neutral country that will never be tempted to use it." Herr Doktor Knutter's tone made it clear that even though it was phrased as such, this was not a question.

"Surely Herr Doktor Knutter, if we will never use it, then there is no reason for us to have it. Nothing good can come of it, only bad things like the way the Americans accidentally shipped it to how many laboratories we can only guess. We should destroy it."

Knutter sighed and silently prayed to the Almighty for the blessing of patience. He strolled to a shelf in his office that displayed a few old relics of medieval weaponry, picked up a long knife, and began to polish its handle with his shirt. "There is a saying, Herr Doktor: the threat is stronger than the execution." He stared for a moment at the other man, then finished polishing the handle and put the knife back on the shelf. "Of course, we would never unleash this terror upon the world, but if another country were to threaten Switzerland, this threat could save us from the horrors of war."

"Or it could unleash the next Black Death upon Europe."

"Herr Doktor, herr Doktor," Knutter soothed, placing a friendly hand on the younger doctor's back, "we are Swiss. We don't do those kinds of things."

The young doctor smiled weakly. Of course we don't, he thought. We just steal biological weapons and lie about it. We're the good guys.

ORIGINATION

By the tenth call, Dr. Rigby and his new Deputy Director began to suspect that some of their so-called partners weren't quite one hundred percent sincere, but Dr. Rigby couldn't think of anything to do other than keep calling. "MyPhonio, call our partner lab in Lebanon."

"This is Dr. Khalil, with whom do I have the pleasure?"

"Hello Dr. Khalil, this is Dr. Rigby from the Junior College of American Pathology." Dr. Rigby explained about the super-flu sample.

"And just how deadly did you say it is?"

"We're not sure, but we think it could be worse than the Spanish Flu epidemic."

"Really. My, that was a big goof up, wasn't it? Are you sure you sent us live super-flu samples with the regular inert flu samples?"

"Yes. The alert we sent two days ago specifies the particular vial that must be destroyed."

"We didn't get any alert from you two days ago."

"We sent it to everyone who got one of the super-flu samples."

"Everyone? You mean it wasn't just us?"

"Ummm…no. It was a few more labs than just yours."

"Hold on a minute." Dr. Khalil put the put the phone on mute. "Hey, guys, you have to come over and hear this." When the group had gathered, Dr. Khalil unmuted the phone. "So you say this live super-flu virus sample was not just sent accidentally to our lab, but to other labs too. How many other labs?"

"A few…" Dr. Rigby took a deep breath; he just wasn't good at lying. "Well, a lot, really. But they're all destroying their samples now."

Dr. Khalil pantomimed a mock gasp to the gathered technicians. "You mean you're trusting them to destroy the samples? You're not sending someone to each lab to make sure they're really destroyed?"

"Well…no. We don't have the budget for that. But after all, these are all our research partners. We're all trying to create vaccines and look for cures, we're not trying to…to…anyway, they're all our partners and when they say they've destroyed the virus samples, they've destroyed the virus samples."

"And you believe them?"

"Er, yes."

The lab technicians tried unsuccessfully to cover their laughter. "Excuse me," said Dr. Khalil, "I don't want to be rude, but you don't sound very sure."

"Have you got this on your speaker phone?"

"Yes. My team has to know about this so we can identify the sample and so they know the true seriousness of this situation." A lab technician snorted.

Dr. Rigby looked at his new Deputy Director and slowly shook his head. "Look, we really need you to destroy the super-flu virus sample. It was an honest mistake on our part and we expect an honest reaction from our partners."

"Oh sure, of course, that's very reasonable of you." Dr. Khalil rolled his eyes, causing more poorly-suppressed snorts from his colleagues. "Now that we are properly apprised of the seriousness of this situation, we will destroy it, how do you Americans say, lickety-split!"

Dr. Rigby tried to ignore the tittering in the background. "I'm sure you understand. We can't have this sort of dangerous virus in a lab area that is not one hundred percent secure. We can't have it fall into the wrong hands."

"Like the American lab that shipped it out, eh?"

"Look, stop laughing, this is serious! It's critical for you to destroy that sample and send us the confirmation right away."

"Oh sure, we will destroy it right away and send you the confirmation real soon."

"Please do that."

"No problem, doctor." Dr. Khalil hung up. The technicians broke down in hysterical laughter.

⌛   ⌛   ⌛   ⌛   ⌛

As they prepared to start the second day of calls, Dr. Rigby tried to flash a grin at his new Deputy Director but it came out as a grimace. "We did the first half. On to the second half." He took a deep breath. "MyPhonio, call our partner lab in Lyon."

"Oui monsieur, this is the Director General, Henri Washclouthe. To 'oom am I speaking?"

"This is Dr. Rigby at the Junior College of American Pathology."

"Ah, Dr. Rigby, 'ow good of you to call. Of course we 'ave receivéd your communiqué about the live super-flu virus you 'ave accidentally allowed to be deported from your laboratory to so many parts of the world." He twirled his thin, waxed moustache. "May I remark, 'ow very, very clumsy of you, I am so sorry for you and the reputation of your laboratory and your government."

"Ah, yes, well, Dr. Washcloth—"

"It is pronounced Wash*clowte*, with the accent on the second portion of the name," Washclouthe interrupted.

"Of course, Dr. Wash*clowth*, my apologies. I'm calling to ensure that you have destroyed the super-flu virus sample as we requested."

"And why should we do this?" Washclouthe demanded. "It is only proper, I think, that such old, strong allies as France and America share such technologies and samples. It does not seem proper that one country, even America, should control such things exclusively."

"Well sir, we're naturally worried about it falling into the wrong hands. The more samples that exist, the more chances there are for something to go wrong."

"Yes, nothing would ever go wrong at an American lab," the Frenchman said dryly. "You 'ave amply demonstrated the unique American ability to maintain complete control of such things."

Dr. Rigby coughed. "Um, yes, well, be that as it may Dr. Wash*clowth*, we are most urgently requesting every lab that received one of the samples we accidentally sent out to destroy it immediately."

"What, don't you trust us? We are your allies!"

"It's not a matter of trust, Dr. Wash*clowth*. It's a matter of international safety. The last thing we want is a pandemic caused by this one mistake."

"And you think the French would release this vile vial into the world!"

"No, no, of course not. We would never think that."

"Then there is no 'arm in us keeping the sample, oui?"

"I'm sorry, sir, we have to insist that you and all the other labs destroy it."

"Hmmmph. It is sad to see that you 'ave so little trust for your strongest allies, who 'ave stood by you through so many campaigns. This is an insult that will not soon be forgotten. 'Owever, you will be 'appy to know that the sample 'as, unfortunately, already been destroyed."

"It's been destroyed? You can confirm that."

"Oui," the Frenchman agreed sadly. "Is it not possible for you to send out another box of flu virus samples with the super-flu, eh, accidentally included?"

"I'm sorry sir, but the super-flu program is undergoing a complete overhaul. There won't be any more accidental shipments."

"But perhaps you can send the box of regular flu virus samples again in any case."

"Dr. Wash*clowth*, I'm sorry, but there won't be a super-flu virus in any sample boxes we ship."

"I know that, monsieur, but we, ah," he sighed deeply, "we still need the samples."

"What's wrong with the samples we sent you?"

"Ah, well, yes, the samples you sent us. The samples you sent us." The Frenchman remained silent so long that Dr. Rigby thought they might have been disconnected, then Dr. Washclouthe finally continued, "There was an, 'ow do you say, an unfortunate incident at the lab with the flu virus samples. They were all accidentally destroyed. Even the super-flu virus," he finished sadly. After a moment, he continued, "It's not fair. Everybody else has it except us."

"So the super-flu virus has been destroyed?"

"Quite definitely, monsieur. Quite definitely." He sighed deeply again. "Are you certain you can't send out another vial?"

"I'll have the lab send you out a new sample box," said Dr. Rigby, "but don't get your hopes up about the super-flu sample."

"I only request that the same person who packaged the first boxes should be the one to package our new box."

⌛   ⌛   ⌛   ⌛   ⌛

ORIGINATION

By the end of the day, Dr. Rigby and his new Deputy Director had called all 107 of the foreign labs. They delegated calling and confirming the destruction of the virus with the American labs to underlings. All of the labs agreed to destroy the active virus, although one lab misunderstood and sent their sample back via the postal service. It was never seen again.

When The Director of the College of American Pathology saw no news about a deadly viral outbreak, she eventually deemed it safe to return from her "vacation" and found, to her surprise, that her job was still there and nobody was the wiser about the little mishap with the deadly virus. When Dr. Rigby learned of her return, he invited The Director to visit the new lab and packing facilities to inspect all the new safeguards that he and FedShip had instituted.

FedShip also told Dr. Rigby that they had completely changed their procedures and now they were no longer shipping dangerous biohazardous material right alongside the other packages—only more carefully; instead, they were shipping dangerous biohazardous material right alongside the other packages—only much, *much* more carefully. "That's two orders of carefulness more," the FedShip representative had confided to Dr. Rigby. "We thought about being much more careful, but then we decided to go whole hog and be much, *much* more careful."

As they toured the facility and came to the vial-filling operation, Dr. Rigby swept his arm out grandly and said, "It's all state-of-the-art safety and security, we've thought of everything. Nothing can go wrong."

"Nothing?" asked The Director skeptically.

"Nothing," Dr. Rigby replied with a firm nod. They heard the loud crash of a lot of glass shattering. A siren started to blare and red lights flashed.

"What was that?" asked The Director. Her nose crinkled involuntarily and she let out a loud, "Achoo!"

Dr. Rigby and The Director stared at each other. "Uh oh," said Dr. Rigby.

S.L. LEITNER

Weird Scenes Inside the Neighborhood

There's danger on the edge of town
Ride the King's highway
Weird scenes inside the gold mine
—The Doors, The End

Sometimes the inside of a gold mine isn't what one would expect; sometimes there are weird scenes inside the gold mine. Maybe there's a ghost, or a treasure, or a man with a pickax and a persistent tic in his eye. These stories are about people, monsters, and even paintings, finding and creating weird scenes inside their neighborhoods.

Please read the series Creating a Masterpiece, Blanque's Suburbia, *and* Scrimshaw Jones *in that order.*

- *Davi*
  Davi does his civic duty.
- *Secret Agent Emily*
  Emily comes alive.
- *Creating a Masterpiece*
  An artist paints perfection.
- *Blanque's Suburbia*
  A housewife...isn't.
- *Scrimshaw Jones*
  A rock carver redefines motion pictures.

S.L. LEITNER

Davi

My name is Davi. I liv heer, rite in this howse. My mommee livs heer too. My daddee and Sheela arnt heer no mor.

Thoz ar my toys rite ther on the gras. My favrit is my brown horsey. I wood play with them now, but i have to go sumwher.

Davie begins to walk up the littered, broken street. He makes no attempt to keep on the sidewalk, which is cracked and overgrown with weeds and multi-hued flowers. The house he is leaving has no door and no windows. The dull white paint is cracked and peeling. Bits of plaster have fallen from the walls, leaving the inner construction exposed. Also exposed are hordes of termites, busily working away at the decayed wooden supports.

The only other creature to be seen is a gaunt old man, stretched out on the street, directly in Davie's path. As Davie approaches, the old man begins to moan piteously. As if he did not see or hear, Davie steps on the old man's hand as he passes. The brittle bones snap and crunch under

Davie's worn black boot. The old man writhes in agony, but those dead or about to die do not concern Davie. Davie is gone, and the forlorn old man lingers in renewed pain.

> I yuwsd too hav a dog. Its name wuz Radi. Radi didnt hav no hare. Hee wuz good at finding food and owl sorts of uthr neet stuf. But he likd too explor too much. Wun day hee went into that howse ovur ther...

Davie points to the crumbled remains of a Bank of America building. Bright green, maroon, and milk white vines are tangled around it, slowly tearing the building apart. The charred remnant of a fallen tree partially blocks the entrance. It is very dark inside.

> ...and nevur kome owt agen. But i no what happend. Radi wuz got by old man Krownus. He livs in ther and eets wutever koms in, kuz old man Krownus kant go owt no mor. My frend Jimee went in ther too. Hee made himself reel small and sloowshed under the tree. I herd him yeling for mee, Davi, Davi, help mee!, but i new that Krownus had him so i didnt go in.

Davie continues to walk down the street. He doesn't even glance at the next old man he passes, who can't groan his anguish because he is already dead.

There is movement in the gutter. A cat drags itself laboriously toward Davie. Its hind legs are stumps, useless. The cat meows futilely at Davie, pleading for help. Davie frowns, and begins to walk away. The cat wails more loudly. Davie stops. The wailing hurts his head and the cat's hungry green eyes make him feel strange, as if he must do something to help the cat. He picks up a piece of loose pavement and as the green eyes widen in terror, brings it down hard and stops the wailing and ends the pain. One green eye stares sightlessly after Davie as he walks away.

Farther up, in the middle of the street, stands a still, lone figure. Its two heads are also still, listening. Even from a distance, its monstrous height and mass are obvious.

> Thatz old Colossus. Hee got too heds, but neethur of them kan see. Hee heers prittee good, tho. He katches stuff by heering it krawling, woking, or flying. But if yur smart, yu kan bee reel kwiet and sneek past him. But if yur reely smart, like mee, yu pik up a rok and take it with yu. Colossus isnt veree smart, but wen he gets yu, yur got. He dont let go until heez takn a few bites owt of yu and yur good and thrashd. My frends babee bruthr wuz a very big boy and i always stayd away from him, but he wuz got like that. It wuz a good fite and wee all watchd, but in the end the babee wuz bit too many tymz and Colossus wun.

Davie approaches Colossus. When he is close, Davie throws his rock across the street. The rock lands with a loud thud and bounces into some bushes. Colossus leaps to the source of the sound. Davie quietly slips past and leaves Colossus frantically searching the bushes for imaginary prey.

Davie turns right at the next street. The buildings are the same as they are everywhere—crumbling, rotting, eroding into meaningless rubble. All the windows have long been shattered, and the doors broken in. Many buildings are missing walls and ceilings; none have retained much paint. Weeds, vines, and kaleidoscopic flowers decorate the streets and houses.

Among the decorations and cracked walls run termites, spiders, and many hard-shelled insects. The clouds do not glow as they once did and shadows are more regular.

Scavengers and survivors have eaten most of the dead. But undiscovered, twisted bodies still lurk in corners, and there are still those that not even scavengers will touch. Davie wades though the desolation and points to the smashed skeleton of a building on his right.

> Lots of us livd in that ther howse a wile ago. Then wun day wile i wuz gon, the flor and rufe kavd in and killd almost evryoudee inside. Thatz wen i dragd mommee ovur too my new howse too liv with mee. Aniway, therz the steps i gotta go up too get too the building. I hav too doo this evry yeer.

Davie climbs up the broken steps of a building on his left. The building is more whole than any other on the street. Some of the vines have even been cut away from its walls and the path to the door is clear. Davie walks through the empty doorway, which opens into what was once a spacious foyer. It is bare except for four wooden desks. At each desk are an empty chair on one side, an occupied chair on the other side, assorted papers, writing implements, and stamps, and several candles that provide the room's only light.

Davie walks to one of four desks and sits down in the empty chair. The man at the desk does not look up. He is writing on and stamping papers with two hands. A third hand pushes a form to Davie.

Davie fills it out.

ORIGINATION

**Form ID-2099-EXT Simple
38 A.N.
TPR-3857340287**

NAME: _Davi_

DEPENDENTS: _Mee and mommee_

AGE: _Thirty-for. Mommee dont get older._

LOCATION: _My howse_

Davie pushes the form back.
The man ignores it.
Then Davi leaves.

S.L. LEITNER

Secret Agent Emily

Emily waddled slowly across the dead brown grass, trying not to spill the two plastic cups of steaming tea. She reached the small orange table, which was too low even for the two deep-seated, fraying wicker chairs next to it, and set the tea down.

Mabel gave a brown-toothed smile, struggled out of the wicker chair's pocket to sit upright on its edge and said, "Thank you, Emily. I hope you remembered to squeeze in some lemon juice."

"Of course, dear," Emily replied as she eased down to the lip of her chair and picked up her tea. They sipped together in silence, watching the warm, late morning sun shimmering off the bay, bathing the Golden Gate Bridge in a double-halo of direct and reflected sunlight.

Eventually, Emily said, "Well? Aren't you going to ask me?" She leaned out over the little tea table.

"Ask you what, Emily?"

"If anything new happened today." Emily's voice quavered a bit. "You usually ask me if anything new has happened."

Mabel smiled and said, "The tea is quite nice today. What's new, Emily?"

"Well, Mabel," Emily allowed her squat body to slide into the depths of the wicker chair's pocket, "I did get a very unusual visit yesterday afternoon."

"Oh yes? From whom?" Mabel leaned towards Emily to gather the news. "Anyone I know?"

"No. It was from a gentleman named John Parker, who works down at the bank."

"Oh? What did he want?"

Emily struggled to haul herself back to the edge of her chair, leaning close to Mabel. "Well, I'm not supposed to tell anybody. Mr. Parker told me everything in the strictest confidence." Emily nodded her head sagely until Mabel prompted, "Come on, dear, what did he say?"

Emily glanced furtively at the gaps in the peeling boards of the rust brown backyard fence. She looked as far over her shoulder as she could manage, then turned back to Mabel and said earnestly, "The people at the bank are trying to catch a criminal." Emily gripped Mabel's wrist with her left hand, and stared into her rheumy brown eyes. "And they want my help!"

"Good gracious, Emily! That sounds terribly exciting. What must you do?"

"Well, Mr. Parker said that it's all very complicated. Apparently, one of their tellers is stealing money from the bank's accounts, but they haven't been able to catch her red-handed. They need real proof. They have to catch her in the act."

"How do you fit in, Emily?"

"Mr. Parker said they need someone who won't arouse the teller's suspicion in order to catch her. So, they picked me out of thousands of customers—"

"A set up!" Mabel shouted, and clapped her hands together joyfully. "How thrilling! It will be just like *The Sting!*"

"Now hush, Mabel! We can't have the whole neighborhood knowing about this, just me and you. And it's not really like *The Sting*, although Mr. Parker did look a bit like Robert Redford in a red bank coat." Emily smiled wistfully.

"Oh well," Mabel said, "I never really did see *The Sting* anyway. What exactly is your part in catching the crook? What do you have to do?"

"Today at one o'clock I'm supposed to go to the bank . . ."

ORIGINATION

Emily stopped outside the bank's glass double-doors, breathing harder than she usually did after the two block walk from the bus stop. Stay calm, like Jane Marple, Emily thought. She studied her bright red shoes with their large, shiny gold buckles, and pulled her cream colored purse up close to her rounded stomach.

"Excuse me," a tall, middle-aged man in a dark blue suit said. "I'd like to enter the bank, please." He smiled condescendingly.

Emily blurted, "I'm awfully sorry," hastily grabbed the cold metal door handle and hurried inside. She shivered from the sudden chill of the air conditioner and realized she was sweating. She looked up; everyone seemed to look away just as she looked at them. But, she felt, they had been looking at her. They were all looking at her. Emily felt as obvious as a bank robber with a mask and gun.

Head down, she hustled to a table to fill out a withdrawal slip. Friday, April 12, the nut brown date plaque on the countertop read. Emily Turner's most famous day, from now on, Emily thought. Fifteen thousand dollars—half of my entire savings. What an enormous sum of money! Emily replaced the chained black pen in its holder, then tried not to be too obvious about finding the teller with long auburn hair and green eyes, who always wore a yellow rose. In a moment Emily spied the rose artfully arranged in a teller's shiny brown hair and moved slowly into her line, trying to appear as relaxed and natural as she could.

It felt like forever, but finally Emily reached the front of the line. The teller stood smiling down at her. "Hi," she said brightly, "How may I help you?"

Emily thought, how can she be so calm? Aloud she said, "I would like to withdraw fifteen thousand dollars, in cash." Emily was surprised her voice didn't tremble.

The teller looked over the withdrawal slip and Emily's bankbook, punched several keys on her computer, then said, "I'll have to get this OK'd by the manager. It'll only take a moment." She smiled cheerfully and walked into the unknown depths of the bank. This must be when she's doing it, Emily thought. Right under our very noses! I certainly hope they get her and give her all she's got coming.

The teller returned and said, "No problem. Let me run it through the system and I'll have your money in just a second. Are you sure you want cash and not a cashier's check?"

"I'm sure," Emily replied curtly. What is she really thinking about behind that pretty, white-tooth smile, Emily wondered. I bet she thinks she's hooked another sucker. But not Emily Turner! This time it will be you in the fisherman's net, my dear.

Two minutes later, Emily hurried down Mission Street, the money stuffed into an envelope inside her tightly clutched purse. Her heart raced like never before; the fast pace made Emily feel flushed with excitement. I'm alive, she thought, I'm alive, I'm alive, I'm alive!

Emily reached the corner of Ocean Avenue and stopped. She hadn't waited long before a low voice behind her said, "Do you ever swim without a lifeguard?"

Emily turned to face a man of average height, wearing a long gray trench coat, a brown fedora and dark sunglasses. Her whole body trembled as she thought, this is it. He's the one. "Only in sunny weather near the wharf," Emily replied, as she had been told by Mr. Parker.

"Emily Turner?" the man asked.

"Yes," Emily answered, hardly daring to breathe. She felt as if the whole scene were playing out like a movie script. "Agent Neville Warwick?"

The man nodded slightly. "You have the catch of the day?" He reached out a black gloved hand, palm upward. Emily dug frantically in her bag, grabbed the envelope from between some coupons and placed it in the agent's hand. "I hope you…I hope you send her up the river," Emily told him. "Those kinds of people don't deserve to live in America."

The man in the trench coat smiled. "Mrs. Turner, it is good, innocent Americans like you who make our job possible."

"You know," Emily began, but the man had already turned his back and was fading into the crowd.

⏳   ⏳   ⏳   ⏳   ⏳

ORIGINATION

"**D**id they get the crooks?" Mabel asked when Emily returned.

"I don't know yet, Mabel. Mr. Parker said he would call me back when something happens." Emily plumped down on the good half of her worn, torn, olive green sofa. "Oh, but it was so exciting today! I went to the bank—would you believe, Mabel, that the crook looked just as sweet as an angel from heaven! Why, she smiled so nicely at me all the time, and no wonder! She thought she had another target—"

"I think you mean a mark, dear," Mabel interrupted.

"Yes, of course, another mark. But not Emily Turner!"

"So did you get the money?"

"Oh yes, I got the money and I went to meet the secret agent."

"Oh my, Emily! That must have been so exciting!" Mabel said, her round little face flushed red with the thought of meeting a government agent. "Was he tall, dark, and handsome? Did he look like Humphrey Bogart?"

"Let me tell you Mabel, I was so nervous! I didn't know my head from my toes! He was so calm and cool."

"Just like Bogart," Mabel said dreamily.

"He came up behind me and whispered the secret passwords to me, and I said mine back, just like in the movies! Then I called him by his… his…"

"Code name?" Mabel prompted breathlessly.

"Yes! His secret code name—Neville Warwick. I wonder what that means in secret FBI talk."

"Or maybe he's from the CIA, Emily. Who's to say?"

"Oh, Mabel! I'm just so excited! Nothing like this has ever happened to me before. I feel so much energy and life—I feel young again!"

"Oh Emily, I can feel it too! I haven't seen you so worked up since that nice Ronald Reagan got elected. I think we should open that old bottle of wine we've been saving, don't you?"

"That sounds like a splendid idea, Mabel. Now where was I keeping that? Oh, darn, there's the phone."

"I'll get it, Emily. Go ahead and find the wine." Mabel picked up the white handset and said, "Hello?" then, "No I'm not, but she's right here." Mabel gave Emily a big grin, and said, "There's a man on the phone for you—I think it's Mr. Parker!"

Emily straightened up in her seat, put on her best concerned voice, took the handset from Mabel, and said, "Hello?"

"Emily Turner?" asked a smooth, friendly voice.

"Yes, I'm here," Emily answered. "Any news about the crook? Did you catch her?"

"Well Mrs. Turner, that is what I'm calling about. Our teller is a very crafty lady. She has what we call in our business a criminal mastermind. She is going to be a very difficult fish to catch, but I think we've just about got her."

"Just about?" Emily leaned back into the couch. "You mean you haven't caught her yet?"

"Our teller is no ordinary criminal, Mrs. Turner. She is a wily fox, a slippery snake. We've got almost enough evidence to put her away, but we don't want to pick her up until we're certain we'll get a conviction. This woman has stolen money from many innocent people. We need just one more piece of evidence—what I'm saying, Mrs. Turner, is that we desperately need your help again."

Emily remained silent for a moment, thinking about all the people this woman had hurt, and all the people who would be hurt if the criminal were not stopped. She straightened in her seat—Emily Turner could not let the people of San Francisco down! "If all those people really need my help," Emily finally replied, "then who am I to say no?"

"Who indeed, Mrs. Turner. San Francisco is lucky to have someone like you as one of its residents."

Emily blushed and said, "Why thank you. What must I do?"

"It's very simple, Mrs. Turner. All you have to do is exactly what you did earlier today, then wait for my phone call. It is exactly two-thirty now. I want you to enter the bank at approximately three forty-five, withdraw the rest of your savings, then meet agent Neville Warwick at four o'clock on the same corner, Mission and Ocean. You will have a new password this time, though. He will say, *The undertow was severe near the wharf today.* You are to respond with, *Yes, I was almost pulled under this morning.* Now repeat your line to me."

"Yes, I was almost pulled under this morning," Emily repeated.

"Excellent," Mr. Parker said. "As with your other funds, we will have to hold this money as evidence until after the trial. Naturally, you will be compensated for your invaluable services. I will contact you again either tonight or tomorrow to give you a progress update. And thank you very, very much, Mrs. Turner."

Emily smiled and said, "I'm glad I can help."

"So are we, Mrs. Turner. Good day."

"Good day." Emily clicked the off button on the handset and gave it back to Mabel. Mabel replaced it, then said, "For goodness sake, Emily, don't just sit there and grin, tell me what the man said!"

"He said I was the only one who could help them. *Me*," Emily said.

"Why, that is just fantastic, dear! Who would imagine you right in the middle of spies, catching crooks and bringing them to justice! Do they want you to…to crack another case, Emily? Are they calling on you to handle another tough one?"

"No, Mabel, it's still the same case. They need more evidence to… to…"

"To nail her!" Mabel crowed, pumping her fist.

"Right!" Emily agreed. "I'm to go to the bank again…"

Mabel was still waiting when Emily returned.

"Well, I guess that was it," Emily said as she settled into her old yellow high-backed chair. "Agent Neville Warwick said now they had enough evidence to get her." Emily sighed.

Mabel glanced at the floor, then at Emily. "Well dear, it's probably best that it's over—too much excitement isn't good for the heart, you know."

"I suppose. But, oh Mabel, I've been having such a grand time!" Emily's eyes watered. "I was really *doing* something!"

After a moment Mabel stood, looked at the dull green carpet, and shuffled toward the door. "It's good to be alive, I guess," she mumbled. "I'd better be going home for dinner now, Emily. Get myself back into the ordinary humdrum."

"Mabel!" Emily called after her, "Don't you want to wait for the phone call? Hear about how they catch the crook? You can stay for supper if you like."

"Well Emily, I don't know…"

"Oh, come on, dear! We'll just have one more bit of excitement before this is all over. Then we can go back to the normal routine."

"Oh, you win, Emily." Mabel smiled. "Let's wait for the phone call."

⧗   ⧗   ⧗   ⧗   ⧗

Three days later, when Mabel was visiting again, the phone call finally came. Emily answered it and said, "Yes, this is Emily Turner." After a few moments, she said, "His name is Mr. Parker and he told me about the criminal bank teller."

Mabel watched as the color slowly drained from Emily's face. "What is it, Emily?" Mabel asked. "You look like a ghost walked over your grave."

"Mabel…oh, Mabel…" Emily's head sagged and she allowed the phone handset to slide back on its hook, "John Parker doesn't work at the bank."

"Oh, I know, Emily. He's really an undercover agent."

"The people at the bank have never heard of John Parker." Emily looked up into Mabel's blank face. "Never." Emily shook her head, tears starting to drip from the wrinkled corners of her grey eyes.

"Maybe he uses a different code name when he's at the bank," Mabel suggested.

Emily sniffled. "The bank officials said I should call the police. I told them about their teller who is a crook, but they said I was wrong, that she wasn't a thief and…and that I should call the police."

Mabel was silent for a minute, her eyebrows drawn together, before she said, "Emily, I think the secret agents must have arranged it to happen this way. After all, they can't be too public."

"Mabel," Emily said, then took a deep breath, "The people at the bank said I was the victim of fraud." Emily's voice shattered. "A c-c-con man game. I'm ruined. It's all gone…" Emily trailed off, then broke down and cried, leaning heavily against Mabel, holding her.

"Oh, Emily, I don't know what to say." Mabel gently patted Emily's back. "I can't believe anyone would do something like this. Now I'm about to cry too. It seems so unfair—why you?"

"Mabel," Emily said, as she pulled away and sat up straight, "why don't you go ahead and go home. I think I want to be alone right now." Emily's gaze fixed on a spot on the dingy white walls where a chip of plaster had fallen away, exposing the rough sheet rock underneath.

"Emily, it's alright. I can stay if you like. I don't mind."

"No. No thank you, Mabel. I…I need my peace right now. I've got to think about what I'm going to do."

"Well, all right, if you think so." Mabel stood slowly and trudged to the door. She opened it, then hesitated on the threshold. "If you need me, Emily…"

Emily managed a brief smile. "I'll see you tomorrow, Mabel."

"Good. See you tomorrow, Emily." The door closed, shutting out the world.

Emily sat silently, reflecting upon all that had happened since Friday morning. All that had happened so very quickly, without time for an old woman to think. Emily's head sank into her mottled hands.

She remembered John Parker's visit, transforming her world's serene dullness into an exciting cinema show of criminals and government agents. How proud she had been, telling Mabel all about it, how thrilling it had been, allowing the cloak of espionage to enshroud them both. She remembered the trembling excitement of the rendezvous with the false agent. And the call from Mr. Parker…she was the only one in the world who could help. Then a weekend of waiting, climaxed by the disillusioning phone call from the bank, and the crushing realization that her life savings were lost.

Emily's head slowly rose from her hands. Her eyes were dry, but distant. The cost was high, she thought, but maybe, just maybe, it wasn't too high after all. What could I have done with it anyway—no one to leave it to; or maybe I'm too old, too old… Emily's thoughts turned inward, experiencing again and again the exciting thrills of Friday, April 12, when Emily Turner was a secret agent.

S.L. LEITNER

Creating a Masterpiece

Please read the series Creating a Masterpiece, Blanque's Suburbia, *and* Scrimshaw Jones *in that order.*

"What are you doing?" I ask Tommb. Tommb believes he is the greatest artist of all time, surpassing Picasso, Dali, Van Gogh, or anyone else you could name.

Tommb ignores me and my question. He kneels and opens his battered black trunk. Graffiti in fluorescent yellow and orange glows faintly in the flickering candlelight of his studio. *PARIS, '84!* in large orange capitals, and the slogans *Biafra lives in 3 million butchered hearts* and *Life is a state of mind.*

Tommb stands, then turns without bothering to close the trunk. His long, thin arms clutch a tempered glass palette and a bunch of dented, silvery tubes. He drops everything on an overturned packing crate in front of me, seizes his last canvas, a 3' by 3', and sets it on his easel.

"Pick a color," he demands.

"What?"

"Or a non-color. Anything you like."

I stare at the oil paint tubes. Each is a universe of color. Cadmium green, cerulean blue, Hansa light yellow, ivory black. I look slowly at Tommb's perpetually flushed cheeks and the sparse brown beard that traces his jaw line until it erupts in scraggly wild abandon from his chin. His sparkling blue eyes reflect dancing streaks of light from the red and orange candles burning in every corner, on every surface, and in every nook of the room. As our eyes meet, I feel strangely compelled to choose. I whisper, "Blue."

Tommb's eyes narrow to laser lances. His upper lip twitches. "Blue," he mutters, eyes darting from paints to canvas to candles to me. "Do you mean simply plain blue? You don't want sky blue or aqua blue?" Tommb picks out the silver tube marked *Blue* and thrusts it before my eyes. "Not indigo or burnt blue? Just blue?"

"Just blue."

Tommb gazes at the blank canvas and becomes still as a glacier. Just as I'm about to prod him, he nods almost imperceptibly and says, "I gave you the choice." His eyes widen and he grins like a wolf. He grabs his palette and squeezes out the whole tube in a continuous blue serpent.

"What are you doing?" I repeat.

Tommb pauses and studies me. His left eyebrow rises slightly in a gesture of contempt, as if his conduct obviously reveals his purpose. "Creating a masterpiece." His tone of voice adds the *of course*.

I ignore Tommb's inference that I am a complete idiot and ask the question that will determine whether I stay or go: "Are you going to meditate before you begin?" To watch Tommb meditate is to experience the zenith of boredom. He sits cross-legged on a burgundy carpet, with only two candles lit, in total silence. Any distraction incurs a hot candle-wax dousing.

"No." Tommb strides to the canvas. "I visualize my painting perfectly." He dips his brush into the glob of plain blue paint masking more than half his palette. He paints quickly, covering the center of the canvas. Soon Tommb has painted a large blue circle. He steps back to glare at the canvas, snarls, then spits into a pile of oily rags near the door.

"Horrible, wouldn't you say?"

I spread my arms, shrug and give him an eye-rolling *how the hell should I know?* Tommb ignores me, switches to a smaller, stiffer brush, then slowly enlarges the circle. I pull a packing crate over to Tommb's side and settle down for a watching session.

"What is it?"

Tommb smiles. "What does it look like?"

"Why don't you just tell me?"

Tommb stops painting. Our eyes meet as he asks, "Why do you spend so much time watching me paint?"

"Why?" I pause. The real question is, what can I say that will provoke Tommb's sense of artistic indignation? "I suppose I watch you for the same reason people cultivate beautiful flowers."

Tommb raises his thick eyebrows and replies seriously, "I can see a parallel in that both flowers and paintings can be beautiful, but beyond that . . ."

"Consider this," I jab, "anyone may observe and appreciate a bouquet of roses. However, only the gardener witnesses the emergence of the rosebud and the fresh beauty of its flowering."

"But it takes so long for a rose to bloom; yet a bouquet can be experienced in a moment."

"That depends on how closely you examine the bouquet, and how long you inhale its fragrance."

Tommb allows silence for a few moments, alternately studying me and the painting. Just as I suspect I won't be able to get a rise out of him, he says, "Don't you think a painting can reach greater emotional and symbolic depths than a flower?"

I grin slowly. "You tread upon perilous philosophical ground, my friend. The symbolism inherent in a rose—"

Tommb cuts me off by spitting loudly into the pile of oily rags. "Not today, my subversive friend. Time for you to tell *me* something. Are you pleased with the world outside these walls?"

"You're dodging—"

"Are you? Couldn't things be better?"

"Everything can improve."

Tommb shakes his head and says, "If something is perfect, it can't improve, nor can it be improved. It's already perfect."

"Perfection is a theoretical condition. More importantly, perfection is a *subjective* condition. Most importantly, nothing perfect exists."

"As far as instruments can measure, that may be true, but what about achieving aesthetic perfection?"

I laugh. "Aesthetic perfection isn't absolute, it's subjective. One man's view of artistic perfection is another man's view of a ruptured septic tank."

"Yet for what else but perfection can an artist strive?" Tommb walks to his trunk and removes his finest brush. The circle's borders are only two inches from the edges of the canvas. Tommb leans close to the canvas, his aquiline nose only six inches from the paint.

"How much longer?" I ask.

"Hard to say—at least a few hours. Relax; the details take time. Why don't you grab a pillow and stretch out?"

Why not, I think. I select a large, orange pillow embroidered *JIM! BREAK ON THROUGH* with brown yarn, and recline in its soft depths.

⌛   ⌛   ⌛   ⌛   ⌛

I slowly open my eyes; the thin drip candles have lost three or four inches. Tommb paints with swift, sure strokes, his face still close to the canvas. I squint hard, but see no brush in his hand.

Abruptly, Tommb releases his invisible tool and carefully plucks a long, straight hair from his head. He slides it through the paint with infinite care, avoiding an excess or dearth of the pigment. When the quantity and texture of paint on the hair satisfy him, Tommb resumes painting. I can hardly distinguish the difference between this circle and the circle before I fell asleep.

Tommb steps back to review his work. His dark eyebrows draw together as his right hand drops the hair and absently picks at his scruffy beard. A confident grin gradually brightens his features. He raises his palette and tells it, "At last, my friend, I am finished." Then he throws it Frisbee style through the open window, into the cold, quiet night, four stories above the hard asphalt street.

For a moment, neither of us move. I hear Tommb's glass palette shatter when it hits the pavement.

I blink, and wonder for a moment if I'm still dozing. Tommb and his old palette belong together, like Orpheus and his lyre. Tommb gives me no chance to ask; he grabs my shoulders, pulls me to my feet and steers me in front of the painting.

"Well?" he asks breathlessly.

I don't know what to say. Tommb glows like a neon light, grinning mouth half open, eyes wide, radiating sheer joy. He expects some form of praise, but what can I say about a blue circle? I hesitate, then stammer, "It's a . . . it's a circle."

Tommb laughs and claps his hands. "Success! A true masterpiece!"

I wonder what I said to make Tommb so happy. My blank expression exposes my confusion, and Tommb's voice strains with exasperation. "Don't you understand? Of course it's a circle. A *perfect* circle. Not a single flaw." Tommb tenderly caresses his canvas. "I have created the first perfect circle!" He looks at me as if I am a very slow child attempting to solve an exceedingly simple problem. I examine the painting. The brush strokes are strong and individual, yet flow together to create an impression of inner harmony from a storm of paint. The circle's perimeter looks flawless—perfectly continuous, no nicks, not even the minutest bulge. I remark, "I can't see any defects, but how can you demonstrate your painting's perfection without instruments?"

"No perfect instrument exists, so we can't measure a perfect circle to find out if it is indeed perfect. Only the eye of a true artist can measure perfection." Tommb grasps my right shoulder with his left hand. His right arm sweeps toward the painting, inviting my critical gaze to follow. "Look at it again. Now what do you see?"

After a few moments of contemplation, I unwisely say, "It's just a circle."

"It is more than *just a circle*. The circle is perfect, therefore capable of leading to more perfection."

I shake my head. "I don't follow you."

"You don't follow me," Tommb replies, pointing to the painting, "but you can. Come, follow me into perfection." Tommb's eyebrows rise as he beckons me to join him at the painting.

I edge to his side. Tommb eases his fingertips onto the circle. He slowly slides all of both hands onto the painting. He explores the texture of the plain blue oil paint, as if caressing each line of each brush stroke. His gliding hands should disrupt the paint. They do not. Tommb closes his eyes; his shaggy head tilts back in ecstasy. The flickering candlelight casts shadows of Tommb's head dancing across the painting. I feel as if I'm observing a mystic ritual.

Now Tommb eases his hand into the circle. Not on the circle, but inside the circle. His hand should break through the cloth of the canvas, but it does not. He slowly works his right arm into the painting up to his elbow, as if he has to push a hydraulic shock absorber on the *other* side.

Tommb smiles. He grabs the easel with his left hand for balance and lifts his right leg. His toe touches the painting, hesitates, then slides past the paint. His ankle, his calf, his entire leg and right shoulder follow easily. Tommb turns his head and looks at me, almost half his body engulfed by the painting. His blue irises twinkle like the shiny blue oil paint on the canvas. "Come," Tommb entices, his voice low and trembling, "follow me into perfection!" Tommb ducks his head effortlessly into the circle. His left shoulder, left arm, left leg, and finally the toe of his left foot disappear.

Tommb has vanished.

I stare at the strange blue circle. The painting, moments ago a mere curiosity, has transformed into an ominous portal. I edge back, eyes locked on the portal, and almost fall over an upright packing crate. Through the thick fuzz of confusion encasing my head like a foam helmet, I hear the thud of the packing crate crashing to the floor. I am not hurt, but my breath comes in short gasps and I can hardly stand on my suddenly gelatinous legs. I glance to my left at the open window and realize I need fresh air. I walk backwards to the window, my gaze fixed on the circle. Will Tommb suddenly thrust his head through the painting like a perverse jack-in-the-box?

I turn and lean out the window. It must be later than I thought. Street lights shine bright, but cars four stories below remain motionless, their owners sleeping in dingy apartments surrounded by cracked plaster walls swarming with roaches. The cool night air smells fresher than the daytime smog, even though it is still the same city air.

What happened to Tommb? Is the circle the gateway to perfection? To paradise? I inhale deeply. Did Tommb really go *through* the painting?

I saw him do it.

But what should I do about it? Can I follow him? Do I want to follow him, and should I? Questions flit across my mind like the moths buzzing around the street light below. No answers; just a blinding ball of strangeness. I knock on the ostensibly solid wooden window frame. Perhaps I should report this to some authority. But who should I tell, and what could they do about it anyway? They wouldn't believe a word.

ORIGINATION

An old Plymouth steel tank across the street cranks over and roars to life. By the street light I see a cloud of blue smoke spit from its exhaust, then break apart and blow away, a universe created and dissolved in an instant.

Maybe if I told other people about the painting they would believe me, and try to follow Tommb into perfection. But would perfection remain perfect once infiltrated by a horde of imperfect humans? If the newcomers transformed Tommb's perfection into ordinary imperfection, it would destroy Tommb.

Perhaps I alone should follow Tommb, leaving no clue as to the true meaning of the painting. But what if Tommb's perfection were not my perfection? Would I be able to return?

I take another deep breath and smell something that is not the oily exhaust fumes of the Plymouth, nor the lingering residue of daytime smog. I turn and face the circle. To my horror, a trail of fire leads from the overturned packing crate past the right side of the easel to the door. One overturned candle still burns next to the blazing crate. Another rests on the fiery remains of Tommb's burgundy meditation rug.

I run to the sink, searching for a bucket. I glance back just as the spreading fire reaches the pile of oily rags. I hear the whoosh as the pile bursts into flames, blocking the door and igniting the cheap plaster and particle board wall. I cannot find anything larger than a drinking glass to hold water. Next to the easel, a packing case full of Tommb's old clothes catches fire.

What should I do?

I rush back to the window. Four stories seems too long a drop to survive. Or is it? The old Plymouth is gone. I see no one in the streets, no lights in the windows of the other apartment buildings.

I turn and behold again the painting.

S.L. LEITNER

Blanque's Suburbia

Please read the series Creating a Masterpiece, Blanque's Suburbia, *and* Scrimshaw Jones *in that order.*

I just lost a friend.

Oh, I don't mean he's dead or anything like that. I just lost him. Or maybe it's more accurate to say he lost me. Perhaps I'll just be diplomatic and say we lost each other. You see, my friend painted a perfect painting, then something weird happened, and . . . and . . . and, well, I lost him.

So now I'm strolling past picture-postcard houses, white and clean with pastel trim, on the way to visit my friend Blanque. I'm a bit unnerved—last night was the third night in a row I couldn't sleep, the third night since I lost my friend.

Suburbia's beautiful early afternoon tranquility massages me like a psychic salve. School's rubbery arms still enfold the kids. Manacles of obligation chain breadwinners to workplaces, while stay-at-homes serenely digest their lunches.

It *is* beautifully quiet. Even the dogs and cats can't think of anything noisier to do than take a nap. I can. The record player in my head selects the live version of the Talking Heads tune *Once In A Lifetime*. The song asks, "Well, how did I get here?"

"À la hoof," I answer as I walk up the driveway of Blanque's pristine house. The close-cropped lawn, immaculate beds of precisely arranged flowers, and perfectly trimmed hedge scream that an anal-retentive family with a terminal case of dullness is busily acting out the American middle-class dream.

Little could be further from, yet closer to, the truth.

The doorbell's ding-dong sounds the same as every doorbell in the neighborhood. Blanque opens the door, greets me with a plastic smile and ushers me in with a wave of her hand. "My, is it two already?"

The apologetic tone sounds about right. It matches the floral print dress, bobbed brown hair and slightly overused red lipstick and foundation. I answer, "You know I don't wear a watch."

"But you always seem to know anyway." The plastic smile again. "Please, come into the living room. Have a seat."

The matching coral couches and armchairs look bright and overstuffed, like sweaty people in Hawaiian shirts at an all-you-can-eat buffet. The spotless material, shiny, *sheeny* clean, gives the impression that no one ever sits there. Blanque bustles off to the kitchen, calling out gaily, "Would you like something to drink? Iced tea? Coke? Coffee?"

"Jack Daniels."

Blanque pokes her head around the corner leading to the kitchen. "You're not playing fair. You promised you'd stay in character and you haven't even been in character since you set foot in the door."

"Since when have *my* promises meant anything?"

She laughs. "How about a beer or some wine? I don't have any of the raw stuff left. We thrashed it all a couple of nights ago."

"Beer." Blanque returns from the kitchen and hands me an open bottle of cold Longboard. I follow her through the showcase living room into a short hall. At the end she opens a door, revealing more hall. As she crosses the threshold, she unzips the print dress. Hardly breaking stride, she whips off the dress and her bobbed brown wig and hangs them on a peg on the wall. She shakes her head as if to toss her untossably short red hair, then grabs a baggy emerald green jumpsuit from the next peg, walks into it, and zips up.

"I hope that set wasn't what you wanted to show me."

"Don't be silly. That's what I show the neighbors."

"What are you going to show me?"

"If I could tell you about it, then it wouldn't be performance art, would it?"

"Of course not. It would be something intelligible."

"Always so polite and accepting, and most of all, *encouraging*. That's what I like about you." She opens a door painted solid scarlet on the left side of the hall.

"Garish," I comment. "Where's the beast's head knocker?" She laughs and waves me into the room. I ask, "Is it part of the performance?"

"The door?" She laughs again. "No. I'm the performance. I'm the artist and I'm the medium. In case you're still confused," Blanque pokes me in the chest, "you're the audience." She points to a solitary olive-colored armchair with a faded pattern, ten feet from a glaring pool of light. The spotlight is the only illumination; the armchair is the only other object in the room. I skirt the edge of the circle of light, reluctant to step through. Silly superstition, like the way I sometimes avoid stepping on the cracks in pavement; still, I follow these feelings when they come.

In contrast to the bloated sofas in the living room, this armchair's padding is worn, comfortable. Blanque closes the red door; on this side, it is unpainted pine.

Blanque steps into the center of the light, facing me. "Welcome, my friend. Today I will take performance art to a new height, a new world, a new universe of reality and perfection. I chose you as my audience because you are my rudest, least cooperative friend." She raises a hand to stop my half-hearted protest. "If I can draw *you* into my world, I can conquer any audience.

"Most artists use a medium beyond themselves," she continues, "paint or stone or paper. Most artists use props—brushes, chisels, pens. But I am not most artists." Blanque stalks the perimeter of the circle of light, then whirls to face me again. "My medium is what you see before you—me. My props are my words, my actions, my expressions, and our imagination, yours and mine."

"But I have no imagination." I grin. Why can't I help saying things like that?

"You know you do, and I'm going to drag it out of you whether you like it or not. Because your imagination is one of my brushes, one of my pens. Without it, you can't come with me, and without you, the performance is meaningless."

"Now *there's* the artsy-fartsy double-talk I expect out of you."

"And you love it, don't you?" Blanque returns to the center of the light. "For this to work, you must focus on me, completely, totally, universally. Every fiber of you must focus only on me," she says, pointing to herself. "In all other forms of art, the medium must inevitably overpower the artist, inevitably outlive the artist's performance. Today, the artist will overcome the limitations of the medium, even though that medium is the artist herself, and by overcoming, expose a new universe as the artist herself overpowers the medium herself."

Blanque opens her arms wide and shows me the grin of a hungry cat. "You like it dark," she purrs, "and I like it dark. In this room, it is dark. The only light is rippling wind." She whirls, the jumpsuit rippling with the motion. Words spill from her throat in urgent haste. "The scent of pine, the darkness of deep green bowers, the decay of spongy leaves beneath naked feet. Feel the crumbling rot between your toes, smell the fetid earth." She is kneeling, scooping air and lifting it to her as dirt. I squeeze the bottle of Longboard, inadequate compensation for being subjected to this performance, but infinitely better than nothing.

"Even in daylight darkness reign; even in rain the air not cleansed; to darkness there is no rein."

I hate it when Blanque tries to be clever like that. She always fails. I'm really not as nasty as she believes or I'd tell her what I think at this point. I do remain thankful for the beer.

Now she stretches toward the ceiling, pirouettes, stretches again, dancing the circle's perimeter. "On all sides, dark, craggy limbs draped in smothering, cloying green decay snake from thick boles of giant trees, reach like blotters to obliterate the sky, reach like ice to leech the heat." The cold from my beer races up my arm and makes me shudder. Or is it just slightly cooler than it was a moment ago?

"One narrow path between their cancerous sweet corruption, one narrow path." A pirouette takes her to the center of the light. "Blindness is the path between all dark," Blanque proclaims. "Yet not to see is also to remain in darkness. The path between darkness and darkness leads only," Blanque spits the last words at my face, "to evil and death."

Yeah, yeah. We made up scarier stuff around the campfire when I was a runt. My beer is the closest thing around here to dead.

Blanque runs around the perimeter, leaps and cries, "Who knows what dreadful beast lurks beyond the edge of light?" She spins and kneels before me. I grin, wondering if she intends the symbolism. Blanque continues in a tone cold and even. "But I go on into night, the night of daylight, beyond the edge of reason." Our eyes lock. The light seems to dim. The room narrows to the universe of Blanque's endlessly deep pupils, black and pure paths of darkness. "I leave the scent of sweet rotting death for the steely fragrance of frigid shadow. The path once living is now dead, a tunnel, its cold gray walls laced with rivulets of water tracing veins in the stone. It crowds closer as I venture into its darkness, narrower and narrower still as the light dims."

And again the light seems to dim. Blanque's eyes glow with the sateen sheen of the overstuffed couches, and in that sheen I glimpse those glistening tunnel walls. "The cold delves below prickling flesh to chill blood as it enters the heart. The moist floor makes no sound as I stalk further, shows no omen of what lurks ahead.

"But I can smell it." Blanque closes her eyes and inhales deeply. Her eyes open, still locked on mine, yet focused somewhere beyond. "The tunnel narrows even more; the smell grows stronger, a stench of festering meat, of carrion under hot sun, yet born on air so cold it bites my nostrils and stings my lungs. And darker still becomes daylight's night."

I can almost smell something, something rotting, something tugging at the corners of my imagination.

"But what is this?" Blanque's gaze lifts past my left shoulder. I catch myself just as I am about to turn and look too. "The beast of daylight's night, its hide glistening with the tunnel's moisture. Its claws like scythes of doom, its eyes twin infernos, but I know no fear." Her eyes again meet mine, again look through them. "For I shall be its master!"

Blanque whirls to the center of the light, even dimmer now. "In daylight darkness let darkness fall!" Her face radiant with fervor, her voice loud, not shouting but strong, she chants:

> "The beast I see before me, call
> For I am master, you are thrall!"

Blanque takes a step forward.

> "Kneel before me darkness' might
> A storm to make the daylight night."

Her gaze fixes proudly on a point far above my head. Her cheeks burn brighter than the faded pool of light, her shoulders square and stiff.
"I said kneel! Kneel!" Blanque takes a step back and blinks.

> "Kneel before me darkness' might
> A storm to make the daylight night."

The strength fades from her voice as the strength has faded from the light. I grudgingly have to admit she is better than I have ever seen her; after the rough beginning she has sucked me in, in spite of myself.
"Kneel!" Blanque's voice has a plaintive edge. She takes another step back, then draws herself up and chants,

> "Begone oh demon of daylight night
> For I am master, now you take flight!"

"Take flight!" Blanque stumbles back, trips over her own feet and lands on her butt. She scoots back to the edge of the light. I can't help whispering, "Great stuff, Blanque!" even at the risk of spoiling the carefully constructed mood.
"Stop it! Go away!" Blanque scuttles along the perimeter of light as if it were a solid wall, her face tight, eyes large, lips thin. "It won't stop! It's coming for me, it sees right through me! Oh, God, help me!" Blanque somersaults across the circle to the opposite side. An unnecessary show-off move, but I'm kind of hooked. "It won't do what I say! It won't do what I think! This isn't supposed to happen. Please stop, please stop!"
Blanque's eyes widen, her lower lip trembles. A tear trickles from her right eye and tumbles down her cheek. I wait, but she doesn't move, doesn't say anything. "Hey Blanque, come on. If you expect me to stay with you, you've got to keep telling me what's happening—this is a good effect, but you can only get away with it for a few seconds."
"Didn't you hear that?"

"Hear what?"

"Didn't you hear it tell me I can't make it stop?"

"No. Come on, I'm actually getting into this—don't lose me now. Tell me what's happening. Oh, wait a minute." I lean forward in the armchair and nod at Blanque. "I get it. It's a way to draw me deeper into it. Pretty tricky!"

"Didn't you hear it?" A frayed edge of panic laces Blanque's voice. Her back presses flat against the imaginary wall between the circle of light and the darkness. She whimpers convincingly. Against my will my heart beats faster and I realize I'm gripping the chair's arms too tight.

"It's towering over me." Blanque shrinks into herself like a sunflower after dusk. "It's bending down. Oh God, it smells like sour milk and green meat.

"Its hide looks like a snake's scales but wetter, slimier. Something's dripping from its fangs, something red. And its breath—oh God!" Blanque shrieks. She ducks her head and raises her arms. I hear fabric tear. A rip appears in the sleeve of her green jumpsuit and a gash paints her forearm with a dripping, vivid crimson crease. Blanque's mouth opens; at first no sound emerges, but then she screams, burning in my brain an afterimage of stretched skin and helpless eyes reflecting primal terror. Then her body is yanked into the air like a marionette; her head vanishes, and blood gushes to the floor, then rapidly the rest of her body vanishes with a spray of bright blood that somehow stays within the circle. The light fades to complete darkness. I knock over the remains of my beer as I stumble to the light switch near the door. It's already on. I rapidly flick it off and on, but there's still no light. I jerk the door open. Light spills into the room. There is no more circle of light, only light fading uniformly from the doorway. There is also no more Blanque, just blood, so much blood.

I look from the dark, empty room to the cheerful splash of inviting light spilling from the open doorway, then back to the dark, empty room. I back out of the room, close the door, stare at the red-painted portal, and realize I just lost another friend. Then I turn and sprint down the hallway as if the Devil himself is chasing me, the harsh scrabble of claws on the other side of that garish scarlet door ringing in my ears.

S.L. LEITNER

Scrimshaw Jones

Please read the series Creating a Masterpiece, Blanque's Suburbia, *and* Scrimshaw Jones *in that order.*

The Seven Scrimshaw Trails have been calling Etcher ever since he read about them. Or so he keeps repeating on the flight to Albuquerque. "The rock carvings scattered along the trails are *exquisite*," Etcher claims, his white-blonde man bun bobbing as he turns to me. "The great Scrimshaw Jones carved all of it. He's one of the foremost unknown Native American and Black artists."

"Foremost unknown?" I reply and treat Etcher to an exaggerated smirk. "Isn't that an oxymoron, like jumbo shrimp or only choice?"

"You know what I mean. Nobody I know in the local carving community has seen his work in person yet and I'm going to be the first."

"They're probably old Native American art. I bet Scrimshaw Jones didn't create any of them."

"I bet he did! I've *seen* pictures of his carvings and read about him in art blogs." Etcher leans over and crowds my arm off the rest between our seats. "One blog said they call him Scrimshaw because the carvings are so fine they look like etching in bone. The thing is, because they're native carvings, it's only a matter of time before the government gets involved and nobody will be able to see them. I'm going to take pictures and learn how Scrimshaw Jones did them before that happens."

"I see. You're going there to get schooled by an old fart scribbling on rocks in the desert."

"Carving," Etcher replies, brow furrowed. "And if you're going to be like this whole trip, you might as well not have come. You said you really needed to get away, but you didn't say you'd be a jerk all the time."

I'm also questioning why I came along for the ride. I'll have to weather a lot of artsy-fartsy bullshit along the way and I'm not sure I'm in the mood. On the other hand, when you see one friend climb into a painting as easily as I climb into bed and another friend have a close encounter of the fatal kind with a demon from some other plane of imagination, a change of scenery sounds good. Real good. Especially because Etcher's footing the bill. Or his parents are, anyway.

Etcher says the weird experiences are all in my head, but even if they are all in my head, they're in my head!

I can't get them out because they happened. I'm suffering from paranormal PTSD. And I can't ignore that it might be fun, or at least distracting, to watch Etcher flail as he tries to translate what passes for his art into a tangible living by copying famous rock carvers. If there are any famous rock carvers. How about that; another oxymoron.

⌛ ⌛ ⌛ ⌛ ⌛

We arrive at Albuquerque in the mid-afternoon of a too-hot-to-be-beautiful late spring day. We tote our backpacks off the plane and pick up Etcher's tool bag full of chisels and stuff from baggage claim. A large temperature gauge on the wall tells us it's 96 outside. We decide to take advantage of the airport's AC and eat a tweener meal in a burger and brew place instead of hitting the road right away. Then we rent a boring gray SUV. The car has fold-down seats so we can sleep in the back and Etcher can pocket some of his parents' expense money. Or better yet, spend it at a bar.

By the time we hit the road, it's late afternoon, but there's still plenty of daylight. It's no longer 96 outside; it's 99. God bless AC. We slog through rush hour until we head out of Albuquerque, west on I-40. I doze off. I wake up from Etcher braking as we get off on an exit marked by a sandwich shop that seems to be in the middle of nowhere. It's a frontage road that parallels I-40 and is part of the real U.S. Route 66. Or was, since Route 66 is officially decommissioned. But it's still there in places, and this is one of them. The interstate has signs saying it's Route 66, but those are lies.

It feels different on the real Route 66. Older and dustier, emptier and lonelier. You could wander off into the nothingness and become nothing yourself. Route 66 symbolizes freedom and self-discovery, like the Route 66 of the movie *Cars* and the TV show *Route 66*, even if only for a few miles.

Route 66 has always fascinated me. That might be the real reason I came—to see Route 66. The beautiful rock formations with arches and crags. The carefully laid-out desert landscape from *Cars*, even though it's animated, is the best part of the movie, and I want Route 66 to look like that. It doesn't, at least, not this part of Route 66. "Get a grip," I tell myself. "It's scrub brush, rocks, and dirt. Nothing to get excited about." Nevertheless, I can't stop staring out the window. Nature is true art, not the manufactured constructs of human hubris. Nothing artsy-fartsy here, no perfect paintings or shadowy monsters to haunt me, just arid truth.

An overpass takes us across railroad tracks. The road angles a little to the left to parallel I-40 and runs through more of the ever-present scrub. Soon we reach the town of Grants. The feel changes again. It's still Route 66, it's still old, but it's no longer empty. The excitement drains out of me like air out of a slashed tire. Freedom and self-discovery have left the building, at least for the moment.

⧗ ⧗ ⧗ ⧗ ⧗

It's early evening, the sun's still up, and we stop at a convenience store. Maps emblazoned *Self-Guided Tour of the Magnificent Seven Scrimshaw Trails* are stuffed into a standee whose upper third shows a simplified cartoon map of the seven trails, surrounded by glowing reviews from various local media sources. I wonder if the map's authors realize that "Magnificent Seven" calls back a great Yul Brynner movie that was a remake of an even greater Kurosawa movie.

"Town's really trying to make hay on the back of this Scrimshaw guy."

Etcher shrugs, replies, "It's working," and buys one of the maps.

We drive down the main drag, hunting for a place to get a beer and look at the map. Neither of us is hungry after eating late at the airport, so any watering hole will do. We stop at a rustic-looking bar, which describes pretty much all of the options.

The AC feels amazing. We grab stools at the long, roughly lacquered wooden bar. The place looks like a locals hangout, but what else would it be? The atmosphere is murky despite the once-upon-a-time-white curtains being too thin to completely block the light filtering through the dirt-rimed windows.

Tables are plain rough wood; chairs, more of the same. Sprinkling of patrons in denim jeans, light, long-sleeved shirts to protect against the sun, boots or off-brand sneakers, hats ranging from cowboy to baseball. Men, except for two corpulent, sun-dried tomato women who could've been 30 or 60 shoehorned into their chairs at a table near one of the windows. If we weren't already seated and the AC didn't feel so good, I'd think about moving on to someplace a bit less of a sausage-fest.

The bartender asks what we want. He looks like a retired biker in his black leather vest, its heavy chain presumably leading to a wallet in the back pocket of his Levi's. No smile lurking between his gray goatee and mustache, doesn't look up as he wipes down something behind the bar. Nevertheless, Etcher leans forward and chirps, "Whiskey!" A few people look our way; most keep their heads down and focus on their drinks.

"Well or call?" asks the bartender.

"Uh…I'm not sure. Whatever you think is good."

"Algodones. Rocks or neat?"

Etcher's eyes dart to me. His head inclines as he questions more than says, "Neat?"

The bartender nods.

In an effort to blend in, I take a guess and order a beer from a chalkboard list of New-Mexico-sounding brews. They have names like Kill the Sun and Project Dank that don't tell you much about what they are. I order the Golden Weasel River IPA because it sounds funny and more than a bit crude, and at least I know what an IPA is. The bartender raises an eyebrow and then turns to take care of the drinks.

ORIGINATION

After a moment, Etcher says, "I can't wait to hike those trails tomorrow!" A big grin plasters his unlined, clean-shaven face with its guilelessly happy blue eyes. "Can you imagine what we'll see? What we'll feel, hiking those trails?"

"I can imagine what I'll feel when that beer gets here. Although I'm already regretting not ordering whiskey."

"Oh, you can have mine! I don't really drink it much—"

"Kidding, Etcher, just kidding."

The bartender's fast. He sets the whiskey in front of Etcher, neat in a lowball glass. As the bartender places my pint in front of me, an old geezer with leathery skin the color of smoky red desert dust pulls up the stool one down from Etcher. He takes off his worn, cocoa brown felt hat; flat brim, round dome, two roadrunner tailfeathers sticking out of a hatband made of red, black, and white beads. He places the hat on the bar. His hair hangs down around his shoulders, gray with pops of pepper that haven't gone over to salt yet. A scraggly grey beard and moustache wander over his face. The bartender doesn't ask and the old guy says nothing, but a moment later, there's a glass of tequila in front of him.

As advertised, my beer is golden in color, possibly because of light refracting off the generous supply of yeasty debris floating and foaming in the beer. Etcher stares at his plain slug of whiskey and whispers, "Is this what neat means?"

I nod and raise my glass. Etcher clinks it with his and we drink. Etcher gasps and almost chokes, but I can't zing him because my eyes are bulging and my cheeks are sucking in so far that they're about to cross each other in the middle of my mouth, right over my bone-dry, puffy tongue. This is the hoppy bitter beer to end all hoppy bitter beers. The chalkboard's 60 IBU claim is sheer perjury.

Etcher coughs and grins. "I guess neither of us got what we expected. While you're recovering…" Etcher pulls the map out of his back pocket. He unfolds it and spreads it on top of the bar. Distances aren't well marked; the makers sacrificed precision for cartoonishness and ads. Plenty of ads. It looks like we drive up Route 66 a while, eventually hang a right, drive a while more, and from there can hit five of the seven trails. "If we head out early tomorrow, we can get more than 12 hours of daylight. This is going to be great! I might even carve something!"

The old man a stool down from Etcher freezes for a tick, then keeps sipping his tequila. "I don't know," I say. "Wouldn't that sort of be like going to the Louvre and drawing a moustache on the Mona Lisa?"

"No, no, it's like hanging another painting at the Louvre near the Mona Lisa. I wouldn't touch any of the carvings."

"But you would put yours on the same level as the Mona Lisa."

"No, no," Etcher protests. "I…just think it would be a cool thing to do."

"Sure. And when it turns out this Scrimshaw guy is a fake, the carvings are actually ancient Native American artwork, and you graffitied up the place, what do you think's going to happen?"

"Graffitied up the place? Graffitied up the place? Right, fine." Etcher takes a cautious sip of the whiskey and manages to get it down without hacking. "At least you're admitting Scrimshaw Jones's carvings are like the Mona Lisa—great art."

"I never said they weren't great art. I said this Scrimshaw Jones guy is probably a fake or doesn't even exist. He probably stumbled on some old Native American carvings and claimed them as his own."

"Scrimshaw Jones might as well be a fake," the old guy one stool down from Etcher says in a slow, heavy voice with a tinge of gravel.

Etcher looks at him. "You think he's a fake? What about the carvings?"

"I didn't say he was a fake. Listen up, that's what your ears are for. I said he might as well be a fake."

"I don't intend to be disrespectful, sir, but I don't get what you mean. I've seen pictures. He's a great artist, brilliant even. The level of detail is spectacular."

"Those carvings in the Outback?" The old guy hooks his thumb in the general direction of the door. "They're no big deal. Overrated."

"But the Seven Scrimshaw Trails are famous!"

"Not really. Some blogger who wanted something new to babble about made up a phony legend and the culture creatures pounced on it. Only people like you think it's a big deal."

"People like me?" Etcher puts his hand on his heart in genuine astonishment. "I'm a rock carver too! I just want to see the beauty of Scrimshaw Jones's carvings."

"And maybe add to them a bit," I toss in.

"There's no beauty. There's just carvings in rock made by a bored man who didn't know what else to do with his time."

I stop staring at my beer and look at the old guy. "Why are you bad-mouthing Jones?" I look closer and he stares right back. "Oh…you're Scrimshaw Jones, aren't you?"

"Yeah, I'm the fake who doesn't exist and is just claiming Native American carvings as his own."

"Cheers," I say lamely.

"Cheers," he replies and we both drink, him with considerably more relish than me.

"It's an honor to meet you, sir," Etcher says as he raises his glass. "You're one of America's great artists. And doing wonders for creating awareness around rock carving."

"I'm creating awareness around rock carving, am I?" Scrimshaw Jones takes a swallow that empties his glass. "My carvings weren't meant for all these tourists. I made 'em for other reasons. I can't even go on those seven trails anymore. They've become too crowded with tour buses from Albuquerque. They even widened three of the access roads." He frowns. "They're not even that good; not worth all this bother."

"How can you say that?" Etcher spreads his arms. "You're one of the great Native American and Black artists of our time!"

"Yeah, there are so many of us competing for the title."

Etcher plows on in his naïve, well-intentioned but brain-dead way. "Do you identify as Native American, as African American, or as both?"

"I identify as Scrimshaw Jones." He swirls the cubes in his empty glass. "If you're going to ask dumb questions, at least have the courtesy to buy me a drink."

The bartender is ahead of Etcher's assenting nod, already pouring the tequila. I wonder how many times this guy has bummed drinks off overeager Etcher-types.

Scrimshaw stares at his glass. "I always hated that name."

"Scrimshaw, Jones, or the whole thing?" I ask.

"Scrimshaw." He takes a long draw of tequila. "Scrimshaw is whalebone carving. I don't carve whalebone. I'm a rock carver, not a sailor. Any idiot can see that. But now I'm stuck with the name Scrimshaw."

"Well, I think it's a fine name," says Etcher. He extends his right hand.

"I'm Llewellyn Fletcher."

Scrimshaw ignores Etcher's hand hovering above the empty stool between them. "Llewellyn? Really?"

"That's why we call him Etcher. Fletcher—Etcher."

"We don't call me Etcher! I'm Llewellyn, I'm called Lew," he turns to me, "and you know it!"

"Did you know that loo in England is a shitter?" says Scrimshaw. "You should stick with Etcher. It's not good, but it's better than being named after a latrine."

I suggest, "Let's get another drink, then we can sort out Etcher's name. I don't want to spoil it, but we'll settle on Etcher."

Etcher sighs and signals the bartender. I switch to whiskey and soda and swear off beers with names like Golden Weasel River. Etcher switches to Topo Chico. Scrimshaw silently stays with tequila. After a few sips, Etcher asks, "Mr. Jones, how do you decide which rocks to carve? Are you looking for a certain shape or texture, or a certain type of rock?"

Scrimshaw savors a pull of tequila. "I don't decide. The rock chooses me."

"So it could be any type of rock?"

"It has to be a special rock. But it almost always turns out to be sandstone or rhyolite."

"I get sandstone—it carves pretty easy and lasts. Why rhyolite?"

"If you look at the carvings, you'll see why. Sometimes rhyolite has eyes. Eyes that see and remember everything that happens in the Outback. There's a lot of life in rhyolite."

I say, "I thought the Outback was in Australia."

"There's Outback all over the place. All around us is the American Outback."

We sip in silence until Scrimshaw puts down his glass and declares, "I could use another drink." Etcher dutifully signals the bartender and I empty my glass. As the drinks arrive, Etcher asks, "What sort of tools do you use? Do you use power tools?"

"I use the kind of tools you power with your hands. Chisels, flats, hammers, rasps, sandpaper; same tools anyone uses. I use other tools too, but none of them are battery powered."

"What other tools?"

"The best tool is your mind."

Etcher nods as if he understands, but he doesn't. I roll my eyes and wish I had a pair of shears handy to snip off his man bun. He asks, "What inspires your carvings?"

Scrimshaw sighs and fixes Etcher with a glare. "Look, this isn't some college classroom where we spout bullshit until our ears are packed with it. Ask a sensible question that makes it worth hanging around for another drink."

I try to bail Etcher out. After all, he is buying the drinks and I'm still thirsty. "Ever see anything interesting out there while you're carving?"

Scrimshaw peers at me over the edge of his glass and pauses his drink. "Now that's a sensible question. A good question, even."

I'm expecting more, but Scrimshaw just sips until I say, "Well? What have you seen?"

"A lot. A lot of things you wouldn't believe even if you saw them. I carved some of those things into the rock. Sometimes, the things I see are already in the rock."

"Like somebody already carved them?"

"Like they were always there, from the beginning of time, just waiting for someone or something to see them and let them out."

"Tell us something you saw," says Etcher.

Scrimshaw downs his glass and looks at Etcher. Etcher raises his hand like a good Pavlov's dog and the bartender refreshes Scrimshaw's drink. I'm drinking as fast as I can, but I can't keep up. "There are living things on those trails. Things that aren't human, or maybe once were human but are no longer."

I grin. "Ghosts and goblins! I wonder if we'll see any tomorrow." Actually, I hope we don't see anything of the sort, especially after the weird things I've seen and been through recently, but I can't help poking.

"Mock me if you want. You'll see some of the things in my carvings." He frowns. "You should go in a tour group. Safer that way."

"A tour group!" Etcher shakes his head vigorously. "No way. They probably wouldn't even let me take my carving tools."

"You won't need those," Scrimshaw says evenly. "But it would be good to be with a group led by someone who knows where they're going."

"We have a map," Etcher says, lifting a corner of the convenience store map that's still on the bar top.

"You were about to tell us about ghosts and goblins," I remind Scrimshaw.

"There are no ghosts and no goblins," Scrimshaw says, his voice rising. "There is the Outback. There are spirits. There are forces. I respect them. I work within their will and at their invitation." Scrimshaw takes a long drink. "I had a friend who carved, but he didn't listen."

Just when I think Scrimshaw's going to leave us hanging, he says, "On the day it happened, we were both on the same trail. Not one of those seven trails on your map, just a trail. He started carving a rock that I knew shouldn't be carved. I told him, but he laughed and said all rocks are different but all rocks are the same, waiting for a carver to let their souls out. I told him to be careful about which souls he let out.

"I went up the trail until the right rock called me. When I finished carving what the rock wanted me to reveal, I went back to see what my friend was carving. My friend," Scrimshaw's eyebrows rise and he shakes his head slightly, "was no longer there. His tools and his water and food were there, but he wasn't. Search parties looked for him for a week, then they declared him dead because nobody could survive that long in the Outback without water."

Scrimshaw drinks, lowers the glass an inch, then brings it back for another pull. He stares straight ahead at the Jack Daniels mirror hanging opposite him on the back wall of the bar. In the mirror, his black pupils look like deep caves in the bloodshot white desert of his eyes. "I know what happened to him, of course. The Outback took him. He disrespected it by carving a forbidden rock and the Outback took him. He knew that land as well as I know it; he'd never get lost. And he didn't. He was taken."

"By what?" asks Etcher.

"By the Outback." Scrimshaw straightens on his barstool. "Don't you listen? The Outback took him. It reached down into his soul and took him. No search party's ever finding him."

"But where did his body go?" asks the ever-credulous Etcher.

"How should I know?"

I knock back the rest of my whiskey. "He probably just took the opportunity to run off. Probably owed someone money."

"Real funny guy, aren't you?" Scrimshaw's narrow eyes and tight lips make goosebumps stand out on my arms. "Regular life of the party. Don't know left from right." Scrimshaw drops back the rest of his tequila and smacks the glass down on the bar with a bang. For the first time, the bartender has an expression that I can't describe as bored. He refills the glass with a quick pour that leaves a splash of tequila pooling on the lacquer. Scrimshaw takes another gulp as the bartender refills my glass.

Scrimshaw turns back to me and says, "I've seen things you wouldn't believe, not even if you had a hundred times as many drinks as you have tonight."

"No doubt. If I had a hundred times as many drinks as I'll have tonight, I'd be dead."

"Keep mocking me if you like, but I know what's there and what isn't there. I'll take you to the Outback tomorrow to find out for yourself, if you've got the guts." He stares at us and I'm not sure what to say, then he says, "Maybe I'll even make a new carving, special for you."

"Would you?" Etcher gushes. "That would be amazing! A personal tour and carving from the great Scrimshaw Jones!"

"Yeah, that's what you'll get all right." He reaches over, grabs the convenience store map, balls it up, and tosses it behind the bar. "You can leave your stupid little map behind. I'll take you on a trail that's not on the map."

"You're doing carvings on an eighth trail?" Etcher leans toward Scrimshaw and almost falls off his barstool.

"You really don't listen, do you? I carve on a lot of trails. The idea that there are seven special trails is bullshit. Made up by the blogger whose story started all of this Scrimshaw Trails idiocy. Sure, I made carvings on those seven trails. I make carvings wherever the rock calls me."

"And you want to take us on one of those other trails?" Etcher says, his voice rising in pitch with each word.

"It takes you a while to latch on to an idea, doesn't it? Yeah, I want to take you on one of those other trails."

"You don't have to twist our arms! I came to see the Scrimshaw Trails and study your work, get some inspiration. It'll help me create my own distinctive style."

Scrimshaw stares at Etcher. He slowly takes a long swig of tequila. He turns toward the bar and carefully puts down the glass, then shifts back to scowl at Etcher. His eyes look cold, his face tense. "You think you can just create a distinctive style? Just invent your style on a whim? By copying someone else?"

"No, no," Etcher protests. "I don't mean it that way. I wouldn't copy your style."

"Damn right you wouldn't. You couldn't. Style is you. That's what style is. It's the *way* you do things, what comes from inside, not from the way somebody else does things." Scrimshaw shakes his head slowly, still staring down Etcher.

Etcher looks down at his Topo Chico, and then without looking up, admits, "I don't have one of those, a way of doing things. That's part of what I'm trying to figure out by coming here. I know I don't have my own style, my own way. But if I experience enough great art, it's bound to emerge."

"Bullshit." Scrimshaw finishes his drink. The bartender's in the groove and pours just after Scrimshaw plants his empty glass on the bar. "You can't find what's inside you outside you. If you don't know yourself, how can you presume to know anyone else? How can you take anything from them for yourself, when you know neither? Know yourself, and your style will be right there."

Etcher squirms under Scrimshaw's stare, feeling its heat even though he's not looking. "I'm still figuring things out. I'm only twenty-six for Christ's sake." Scrimshaw says nothing. He picks up his glass and takes a pull, his eyes never leaving Etcher. Etcher squirms more, then snaps, "Okay, okay, so I don't know myself well enough to have my own style. Everybody's on a journey."

I feel kind of bad for Etcher. He meets the guy whose work he traveled a ton of miles to see and the guy shits all over him. Etcher's really not a bad guy, just a little privileged, a little overeager, and gullible. I love playing poker with him, but this is getting rough. I down the rest of my drink and give Etcher a pat on the back as the barkeep refills my glass. "That's right, everybody's on a journey. And most of us are going nowhere."

"First intelligent thing you've said," Scrimshaw mutters.

"How are we going to meet up tomorrow?" Etcher asks.

"Meet in front of this place. Six a.m. You bring the car."

"How about ten for brunch?" I offer.

Etcher turns his head to shoot me a glare. "Six a.m. it is," Etcher says. "We'll have the whole day."

I sigh. "The things I put up with for you, Etcher."

"Lew. My name is Lew."

"Maybe you're wrong to call him Etcher," Scrimshaw says. "If he wants to be called after a toilet, let him."

"Naw, everyone gets a nickname. He's Etcher. And I think I'm going to call you Scrimshawshank Redemption."

"You'll do no such thing. My name is Scrimshaw and if you want me to take you tomorrow, you'll remember that."

"I thought you didn't like the name Scrimshaw. I'm just trying to help you out."

"Doesn't matter if I like it or not, it's my *name*." Scrimshaw downs the rest of his tequila and slams the glass on the bar. He puts on his hat, gets up from the barstool, and faces us. "Don't be late. Bring a car, I don't have one." He turns and stalks out the door.

⌛   ⌛   ⌛   ⌛   ⌛

We leave the bar after two more rounds, my head buzzing from the whiskey. We stop at a fast food joint and then find an out-of-the-way place to park the SUV for the night. We eat in the front seats and talk a bit about the oddity that is Scrimshaw Jones before we pull down the seats and crash. It turns out the six a.m. meetup isn't hard to make because we're both up at five to pee. My mouth is bone dry and my head feels like a block of wood.

We hit another fast food place for coffee, greasy sausage and cheese breakfast sandwiches, greasier tater tots, and a large water for me. We're at the parking lot by six sharp, still working on our mondo-size coffees. Scrimshaw isn't there. With all the tequila he drank last night, did he even remember he was supposed to meet us? We talk for a bit before pulling out our phones and devolving into screen hypnosis. By around seven, the water and coffee are working some magic and I'm feeling better, but I'm running out of things to do. "I'm bored. I'm beginning to wish Scrimshaw hadn't trashed our map."

"Let's give him another half hour. If he doesn't show up, we'll get another map."

A thought forces its way through my hazy mind. "Do you think that guy really is Scrimshaw Jones? Maybe he just says he is to get free drinks."

Etcher's head jerks in my direction. "What? Do…do you think that guy wasn't Scrimshaw? Was he just messing with us?"

"Naw, I think he's the guy. Probably doesn't pay much attention to time or some artsy-fartsy thing like that."

Around seven-thirty, Scrimshaw trudges over from a greasy spoon across the street as if he's perfectly on time, topped by his round-domed brown hat with its flat brim, feathers, and beads. The straps of a heavy pack strain against his shoulders and he's carrying two large, dented metal canisters that pull his arms straight down. He reaches us and drops the canisters to clang onto the pavement and make sloshing sounds. He shrugs out of the backpack, which he places gently on the ground. He doesn't greet us or say good morning. He points to the SUV. "Is that your car?"

"Yes," Etcher replies.

"Good. I'll drive."

"Uh, I don't know. The car's in my name and I'm the only insured driver."

"I'm not good at giving directions. I'll drive."

"But what if we get in an accident?"

"We'll say you were driving."

"I don't know. I'm responsible for the car."

"Fine. You drive and I'll stay here." Scrimshaw hefts up his backpack, slides his arms though the straps, and then reaches for the canisters.

I roll my eyes. "Just let him drive, Etcher. This is what you came all the way here for. And who the hell cares if something happens to the car, it's just a rental. You took the insurance. We could drive off a cliff and they'd bring us a new car, no charge, no skin off your nose."

"That's good," Scrimshaw says as he nods. "Now give me the keys. Otherwise, I have better things to do."

Etcher looks at me, eyes wide, head shaking "no".

I put my hands on my hips and tilt my head toward Etcher. "C'mon. Let's go see some rock carvings. That's what you came for, right?"

After a moment, Etcher's face softens. He reaches into the right front pocket of his Levi's, pulls out the key fob, and hands it to Scrimshaw.

"You two are in the back seat. My tools go up front." Scrimshaw strides to the SUV and unlocks the doors and tailgate. Etcher is about to protest. I shake my head. Etcher deflates.

Scrimshaw throws our backpacks out of the cargo area and onto the SUV's back seat, where we're supposed to sit, even though there's plenty of space for everything in the back. He shoves the water canisters into the cargo area, which still holds Etcher's tool bag. Scrimshaw slams the tailgate shut. He takes his backpack around to the front passenger seat and opens the door. He lays the pack gently on the seat and straps it in with the seat belt, then walks around to the driver's door and gets in.

Etcher climbs in behind him and I take the passenger-side seat. We squeeze our backpacks between us.

Scrimshaw starts the car. He hangs a left onto the main drag without looking for cross traffic or caring about the water canisters bouncing around the cargo area and heads west out of town. No wonder the canisters look beaten up. There's not much traffic, a good thing in light of Scrimshaw's driving habits. From my recollection of the convenience-store map, I figure we have 30 or 40 minutes before we leave Route 66 and head toward the trails.

We get into the town of Milan almost immediately. Instead of driving through, near the far end of town, we take a right on NM 605. The SUV's rear tires skid with the force of Scrimshaw's turn; the canisters bang into the car, Etcher's equipment bag, and each other. I wonder if a canister will break and flood the car. At least our backpacks stop me from sliding into Etcher.

I say to Scrimshaw, "Hey, why all the water?"

"You have to keep the rocks wet when you're working on them. Lots of dust. Keep them wet and you don't have to breathe in the dust."

"Makes the rock easier to work, too," Etcher adds.

Soon we're past the last vestiges of Milan and in old mining territory. The road begins to bank a bit to the right. Scrimshaw tells us we're passing by a place called Poison Canyon. "It wasn't poison before the mining," he says.

A few miles later, we pass what Scrimshaw calls "a major crossroad," which turns out to be a T-intersection in the middle of nowhere with another state road. Scrimshaw says, "I've carved on trails up that way, too, where the San Mateo mesas are. Lots of trails out there. Lots of things happening. But we're not going there today." NM 605 curves harder right and takes us east, into the rising sun.

"Where are we going?" Etcher asks.

"We're heading toward the Jesus Mesa. Don't expect to meet your god there, though." He chuckles. "I don't know if the trail I have in mind is officially on the Jesus Mesa, but it's on it or near it."

"How many carvings have you done on this trail?"

Scrimshaw shrugs. "I don't count carvings. I just make 'em."

About a mile and a half past the "major crossroad", Scrimshaw hangs a violent left onto a dirt road, tires slithering across the gravel. Pressed up against the window, I catch a glimpse of a road sign but it flies by too fast to read. We scrape against scrub bushes and straighten out. I'm not sure if the scrub is growing in the road or if Scrimshaw's off the road, but I do know we're bumping along at much too good a pace. If I weren't wearing a seat belt, I'd probably be launched into the roof every other bump.

"You know, this thing has four-wheel drive," I shout as I grip the door handle.

"Yeah?" Scrimshaw replies, but doesn't shift the transmission.

We drive almost due north as the sun climbs higher on our right, tires spitting gravel all around us. Etcher's man bun bounces like an upside down punching bag in my peripheral vision and I regret yet again the absence of shears.

The terrain looks something like I imagine the moon would look, but with grey and dark green scrub thrown in. Rock, scrub, dust, dirt, gullies, and then more of the same. We drive across two washes that must be from snow melt. The scrub is greener in and between them. As we cross the second wash, we see clumps of bushy-looking trees and a few loners, and a blur that might be a jackrabbit or a roadrunner or maybe one of Scrimshaw's ghosts. Some of the trees come right to the edge of the dirt road. I keep thinking Scrimshaw's going to bounce us into one of them, maybe play pachinko down the road with the car as a ball and the trees as pegs.

The trees, never close to being a forest, thin out and we're back to moonscapes of rock outcroppings with an occasional tree in the distance.

ORIGINATION

The road straightens out, crosses another wash, then takes a ninety degree curve to the right to parallel a deep gully. Scrimshaw keeps the SUV just on the edge of losing the tires' grip on the dirt.

The road curves gently to the right and I unwisely relax for a moment. Then the road hooks viciously to the left and I'm pressed up against the window again with the rear wheels sliding bump, bump, bump across the scrabble. "Four-wheel drive?" I call out hopefully, but Scrimshaw's hands remain locked on the wheel and his eyes remain locked on the road.

The road curves gently again, between a few trees. We reach a fork in the road and take the right tine, which curves into a ninety-degree turn and then joins another dirt track. All these turns; we seem to be taking the most obtuse path possible. If something happened to Scrimshaw, would we be able to navigate back? I check my cell phone and confirm there's no service. I think Etcher downloaded maps to the SUV's GPS, but who knows how accurate they are or if these trails show up on those maps. Or even if the SUV will survive the trip, the way Scrimshaw's driving.

We come to another big turn, this one a brutal twist to the right. It looks like the road runs along the skirt of what I assume is the Jesus Mesa. Scrimshaw should slow for the turn, but he doesn't. I grip the grab handle tight and brace for the rollover. Instead of taking the sharp right and rolling the car like a die, killing us all, Scrimshaw plows straight ahead, past the edge of the road, between two scrub bushes, only probably killing us all. The SUV hits a big bump and goes airborne for a moment, then the tires hit the dirt too much on the front wheels, the SUV fishtails, and the passenger side—where I'm sitting—slams against a boulder. I feel the impact through the door. The crash miraculously rights the car on what looks like the suggestion of a road, or maybe a wide hiking trail.

"Sorry, I forgot about that being there. But it's always fun to get a bit of air."

"You...you just hit that rock!" Etcher splutters.

"Yeah. I just apologized for that."

Etcher leans forward and yells, "I knew I shouldn't have let you drive!" His face turns tomato red. "How am I going to explain this to the rental company?"

Scrimshaw shrugs. "I'd explain that I got the insurance."

"I'm okay," I holler, "in case anyone cares."

We jolt along the trail in silence for a while, climbing the skirt of the mesa. The pissed off look on Etcher's face seems on the verge of setting like a plaster cast. "So is this the Jesus Mesa?" I ask, trying to break Etcher's funk.

"Yeah, I think so, maybe one of the lower parts of it. There aren't any signs, though. If you go the other way on that road, you can get to the top of the highest mesa. But what other people name a place doesn't matter."

"I suppose not." Nothing else comes to me, so I just look out the window. There's more green and more trees, not just the bushy-looking ones, pine trees too. We climb steadily through a wide gorge. A mesa looms on our right, a steep slope up to a ridge on our left. At what looks like a random place, Scrimshaw stops the car and turns off the engine. "This is where we get out."

"How did you find this place?" I ask. "It's in the middle of nowhere."

"I know the Outback. We're in the middle of somewhere, not nowhere. And when the wind kicks up, it gets dusty." He pulls a white bandana out of a pocket in his pack and wraps it over his mouth and nose.

"Do you have any more of those?"

"No."

"Wish you'd have told us to bring them."

"Why?" He turns to fix me with his eyes, somehow a boiling brown framed between the edge of the bandana and the brim of his hat. Sweat breaks out on the back of my neck. "You should wish you thought about where you were going. People who don't think about where they're going don't tend to get there. Sometimes they get completely lost." Scrimshaw gets out of the car, gathers his pack, and takes his water canisters out of the cargo area.

Etcher and I get out and stretch. When I see the crater of a dent that covers most of my door, I'm surprised it opened. The sun's glare reflects super bright off everything, but at least we have sunglasses. Scrimshaw doesn't. I guess the brim of his hat is enough.

It's not even 9:30 a.m., it's already hot, and I already miss the SUV's AC even though we just got out of the car. At least we made it here in one piece, and I'm in no hurry to get back in the car, at least not with Scrimshaw at the wheel. Scrimshaw shoulders his pack, then looks at Etcher and points to the canisters. "I'll let you carry those. I'd let you carry my pack too, but I don't trust you to handle it."

"But I need to carry my tools!" Etcher protests.

"No you don't. Leave 'em in the car. You need to carry water." Scrimshaw stashes the key fob with its plastic identifier tag into a pocket in his pack and then checks the rest of the pack while Etcher stands with gaping-fish mouth and makes incoherent noises. I grab a bottle of water from each of our packs and force them into my pants pockets.

Etcher asks me to grab his tool bag. It's heavy; I sling it across my back as Scrimshaw looks up and glares. Etcher stomps to the canisters and hoists them off the ground. "Jesus! Do you need both of them?"

"You never know how much you need. Besides, if you only carry one, you walk lop-sided."

Etcher looks at me. I shake my head. "Nope. Wouldn't want you to walk lop-sided. Besides, I've got your tool bag to take care of."

Etcher's eyes close for a moment. He gives a deep stage sigh and purses his lips. "Okay…"

Scrimshaw turns sideways and edges between clumps of scrub. We follow and find ourselves climbing the slope on a faint trail we'd have never known was there. Or maybe it isn't there. It often seems like we're randomly zig-zagging up the slope, then there are a few steps that feel trail-ish, and then there's no sign of a trail. Scrimshaw hikes confidently, as if he's reading street signs. We climb, traversing up the slope, through clumps of scrub and around outcroppings of rock. Behind me, Etcher wheezes and the water sloshes in the canisters. He shouts, "I need to put these down for a minute."

"Nonsense," Scrimshaw calls back. "We're almost at the Welcome Stone."

"The Welcome Stone?"

"It welcomes people to the trail. Sets the mood. You'll see."

After several more spurned requests to "hold up for a minute, guys", about two-thirds of the way up the slope, we reach a small outcropping of rock and Scrimshaw stops. When Etcher catches up, Scrimshaw points at a smaller stone shadowed by larger stones. Etcher pants, "Sandstone," as he arrives and puts down the canisters. Sweat drips down his face.

"Take a closer look. You can't see it well in the shade."

Etcher and I kneel in front of the Welcome Stone. The scene carved into the rock shows a path that starts near the bottom of the stone and winds up through images of trees and rocks and bushes. Individual leaves, cracks in the rocks, and even the texture of the bushes and bark and dirt are engraved in fine detail. The closer I look, the more I see. The carved path leads not to a place, but to a collection of meticulously sculpted symbols at the top of the stone. I expected something cruder, but this looks at least as good as art I've seen in museums.

"Gorgeous," Etcher breathes as he takes pictures with his phone. "Such precision."

"What are the icons at the top?" I ask.

"They tell you something is here," Scrimshaw replies. "The bird tracks tell you to keep climbing. The arrowhead warns you to stay alert."

"Why do you need to stay alert?"

"See the wolf symbol? It means the Outback is strong. It protects itself. That's why you have to stay alert."

Etcher asks, "Did you choose this stone because it's separated from the others?"

"Like I said, I don't choose the stones, they call to me. Rock Time changed this one, though. It used to be one with the other stones in this group."

"Rock Time?"

"The stones along the trails evolve, the mountains and valleys evolve, their spirits evolve. But usually too slow to observe. That's Rock Time."

"Oh," I say, "you mean erosion."

"I know what I mean." Scrimshaw stares and points at me with his right index finger. "I mean Rock Time. And it doesn't always move slow, like erosion, and it doesn't always move the same, like regular time. Sometimes it moves fast, faster than you would believe. But you don't understand that yet. Erosion is something different."

I shrug. Just what I need after the way I lost my other two friends, more metaphysical crap.

"Come on," Scrimshaw says. We climb the rest of the slope and emerge onto a rough dirt and stone trail at the crest. It runs both directions up and down the wide ridge, with rocks and scrub bushes lining the path. Etcher releases the canisters to bang to the ground and shakes out his arms. The sun's brilliance is almost too much for my sunglasses; I don't know how Scrimshaw manages to squint through it.

ORIGINATION

"I carved a rock just up the trail a few weeks ago. I'll show you that one first." Etcher looks dismayed that we're not resting and gestures to me, but I'm already turning up the path. We follow Scrimshaw just a hundred yards or so before he stops. I hear the sloshy thunk of the canisters hitting the ground behind me, accompanied by a deep exhalation.

This carving is in full sunlight so we see the fine detail right away. It's a triptych, like a three-panel comic strip. On the left side of the rock face, two eagles battle in midair over the Outback, as Scrimshaw calls it. It looks familiar. I look up and down the trail. The carving matches the landmarks perfectly; too perfectly, as if the artist had somehow seen the eagles from the ridge and seen the ridge from the air at the same time, resulting in a supernatural perfection of art.

In the middle of the rock face, the two eagles fall toward the ridge, talons entangled, wings spread, eyes locked on each other. The last panel shows the eagles apparently hitting the ground, or maybe falling past the ridge into the valley. Their heads peek above the ridge and that's it. "It looks like the story of a dogfight between two eagles." I point at the last panel. "It looks like they kept fighting all the way to the ground. Is this something you saw happen up here?"

"Yeah. But it's not what you think it is."

"What is it, then?"

Scrimshaw grabs a canteen hanging from his pack, pulls down the bandana, and takes a drink. He doesn't offer it to us, so I pull the water bottles out of my pockets, hand one to Etcher, and we open them and drink. "It was two golden eagles fighting, all right, but in the end, they wanted to let go. They struggled hard to let go. But their fight disturbed the Outback. The Outback didn't allow the eagles to let go and they plummeted into the land. The last thing I saw was their heads, just before the Outback took them."

"Don't eagles sometimes fight so ferociously that their claws get caught and they can't separate?"

"That's not what this was."

"Man, you really have some imagination."

Scrimshaw glares at me. "It's not imagination."

Etcher squats to look closer at the carving and take photos. "This is rhyolite, not sandstone, isn't it?"

91

"Yeah. When the eagles fought, it called to me. Rhyolite doesn't call much; only for special things."

"Isn't it hard to carve in rhyolite? There's so much sandstone up here, why not use that?"

"I told you, it called to me. You don't listen any better than you did last night."

I look closer too. Scrimshaw used white-colored "eyes" embedded in the pink-red rock for the eagles' eyes in all three scenes. "Did you decide where the eagles should be positioned based on the eyes?" I ask.

Scrimshaw replies slowly, emphasizing each word. "I told you. I don't decide. The rock decides." I can sense his frown behind the bandana. "It was in the rock before I got there."

"How can that be? If you carved the fight you saw, didn't you decide what to carve?"

Scrimshaw shakes his head. "I only revealed what was already in the rock. If you can't understand that, I can't explain it any better." He turns and looks up the trail. "Come on, I'll show you another one. Maybe you'll begin to get it."

"But how could it be in the rock already if you just saw it?"

Scrimshaw closes his eyes and shakes his head again as he turns up the trail.

Etcher rises, his eyes fixed on the carving even as his body starts to turn. He whistles. "You'd never think you could carve this kind of detail in rock even with power tools." We're already moving on and he hustles to catch up. "I can see why they call you Scrimshaw."

"Didn't you say you hate that name?" I pop in. "How did you wind up with it if you hate it? Or was it your birth name?"

"It wasn't my birth name."

"What was your birth name?" Etcher asks.

"I can't remember. It's been Scrimshaw a long time."

I follow Scrimshaw down the trail, his footfalls light and silent. The sun beats down from mid-morning height, accompanied by the constant sloshing of the water in the canisters and Etcher's heavy breathing behind me. My shirt's soaked with sweat and I wish I'd brought a hat, but my lid is in my pack, back in the car. The rocks on both sides of the trail look pretty much the same, reddish, brownish, and cracked, just as the dirt on the trail looks the same. It's hard to tell how far we've walked because nothing stands out. It's not like there's a 7-Eleven or something on the corner of Rock Avenue and Scrub Brush Street.

Scrimshaw speaks again as if there had been no time between his last sentence and this one. "When I was younger, I'd find small rocks out here, carve them, and then bring them into town to sell at the rock shop. After a while, the shopkeep started calling me Scrimshaw. I didn't like it. I told him what scrimshaw is and what rock carving is, but he kept calling me Scrimshaw anyway. One day I asked him why." Scrimshaw kicks a pebble. "He said my carvings had the detail and feel of *scrimshaw*." His tone makes *scrimshaw* sound like a dirty word. "People picked it up and started calling me Scrimshaw. The more I fought it, the more they called me Scrimshaw. Then everybody was calling me Scrimshaw. So now I'm Scrimshaw. I can't stop it any more than an eagle can stop people from calling it an eagle."

Scrimshaw stops in front of a tall, wide stone and gestures at it. We gather around a large flat section with a carved scene that must be at least six feet wide and five feet high. We all take a drink and Etcher takes more pics. After the last two stones, I can tell that this one is sandstone. Like the two other carvings, the detail is etched with machine-like precision. Yet it's somehow clear that no machine made these images.

Once again, I recognize this ridge running along the bottom of the carving. The rest of the scene looks like a mashup of Munch's *The Scream*, Van Gogh's *Starry Night*, and Tim Burton's *The Nightmare Before Christmas*. Ghoulish creatures, *things*, crowd the skies and flow into the scene from every direction, rising from the ground, diving from the cloud-and-star-streaked sky, flooding in from all sides.

Stretched, bony faces; wide mouths with razor-pointed teeth and eye sockets that seem to glow through the dull red-brown color of the stone. Long arms end at long, diaphanous fingers with claw-like nails, reaching, reaching, reaching. Torsos fade into vaporous trails. Some of the creatures are entangled in the sky over the ridge. Entangled…or entwined? I'm not sure what's going on. Is it a fight? Is it a party? Is it an orgy?

Etcher speaks for me when he asks, "What is this?"

"I saw this one night," Scrimshaw answers.

"You saw this?" I can't keep disbelief out of my tone.

"I was up here one night. I wasn't here to carve. I was just leaning against a rock, listening and looking."

"And then this happened?"

"Yeah."

I mutter, "It's amazing what a bit of peyote can do," intending it just for Etcher, but Scrimshaw's got sharp ears. His eyes blaze as he turns to me. "Now why would you want to say something like that." His words aren't a question, they're a rebuke.

Etcher charges blindly through the uncomfortable moment, eyes on the carving. "It does look like fine etching in whalebone." Scrimshaw's eyes crinkle as he grimaces. "I don't know how you could carve this without precision engraving pens. And with sandstone, even then…you'd need a laser." He whistles. "How did you do this? How did you carve distinct lines so close together without crumbling the stone? How did you get the fading effect? It gives depth while adding spookiness. The blogs were right, you're a genius."

"It's not genius. It's heart," Scrimshaw touches his heart, "mind," he touches his forehead, "and soul," he spreads his arms, "all in harmony with the stone. Listening. Always listening."

"Wow. Wow." Etcher looks at me and grins, then looks at Scrimshaw. "This makes me feel like carving right now!"

"I told you to leave your tools in the car," Scrimshaw says sharply. "This isn't the place for someone who knows as little as you."

"I brought my tools because I knew I would be inspired, and when I'm inspired, that's the time to carve." Etcher stands up. "I might know more than you think."

Scrimshaw glares at Etcher, hands on hips, eyes narrow. Etcher stares back. To my surprise, he holds Scrimshaw's gaze until Scrimshaw says, "I promised I'd make a carving for you. You'll see what it's about." Scrimshaw turns and heads up the trail. I raise my eyebrows at Etcher, shrug, and start walking. Etcher shakes his head, grabs the water canisters, and follows.

Scrimshaw strides fast, arms swinging at his sides. Etcher struggles to keep up. We march a good distance without speaking, marinating in our sweat. Scrimshaw slows as we approach an outcropping, then stops. He cocks his head to the right.

"Is one of these calling to you?" Etcher wheezes hopefully.

Scrimshaw answers by continuing up the trail. He stops at the next outcropping. He drifts toward a rock formation on his left, examining the rocks, slowly gliding by until he stops in front of one. To me, it looks like every other rock in the outcropping, which looks like every other outcropping on the ridge.

"Here," Scrimshaw says. "This is the one."

"Awesome!" Etcher says and drops the canisters. "It's time to see the great Scrimshaw Jones in action!"

"First thing is to get the stone wet. Hand me the water."

Etcher gives Scrimshaw one of the canisters. Scrimshaw unscrews the top, hauls up the canister with both hands, and then pours a stream of water over the chosen rock.

Etcher crouches to get a better look and says, "This one's kind of reddish-pink rhyolite, isn't it?"

Scrimshaw nods as he surveys the rock, dumps more water on it, and then puts down the canister. "Yeah. You see the white eyes in the rock?"

"Yes."

"That means the rock has a soul. It sees out of those eyes."

"O-kay."

"Now we'll wait a few minutes for it to dry a little. There's another carving I want to show you just up the trail. It won't take long." Scrimshaw takes a gulp of water from his canteen and we do the same from our bottles, then we're moving again. After a very short walk, Scrimshaw stops and points to a sandstone rock on the right side of the trail.

Once again, the lower part of the carving is this trail. I wonder if that's Scrimshaw's signature. Or short cut. Two large birds hover over the trail, their wings blurred in flight yet somehow detailed. "What does it mean?" I ask.

"Do you know what kind of birds these are?" he replies.

"No."

"Hummingbirds." As if that was enough to answer the question.

As Etcher takes photos, he says, "They *are* hummingbirds. The beak shape. The wings, for God's sake. It's almost like they're alive."

"Hummingbirds represent beauty and wisdom, two things neither of you possess. But if you spend enough time here, you might be able to get them." He shakes his head. "No guarantees in your cases, but we can try."

"Nothing's gonna help on the beauty side of things," I declare with a smile.

Instead of smiling with me, Scrimshaw shakes his head again. "No, probably not."

After a minute or two, Scrimshaw says, "The water's done its job. The sun's dried it enough." He swings back onto the trail and we traipse back to the chunk of rhyolite that Scrimshaw doused.

On the ground near the rock, Scrimshaw lays out an assortment of chisels, flats, hammers, and rasps, along with a stack of sandpaper of varying grit. He chisels with incredible speed, yet minimal force. The sun hits hotter and hotter. I take another drink and am out of water.

It seems impossible, but in about ten minutes, with Etcher hovering over his shoulder like a pantomime shadow, Scrimshaw chisels the ridge and the trail in perfect detail, including the rock he's working on now. The trail with its rocks and scrub seems to be the focus and consumes more than half of the stone's face.

"I can't stand it," Etcher declares. "Give me my bag."

I unsling the bag and hand it to Etcher. It feels good to get rid of the weight of all those tools, but the bag has left my shirt perspiration-plastered sticky against my back. Scrimshaw looks over as Etcher unzips the bag and starts taking out tools and laying them on the ground near another rock that has a nice, flat face. I see Scrimshaw's eyes widen and imagine I can see the scowl under his bandana. He turns and looks at me, but I don't know what to say. I'm not going to be the one to tell Etcher not to carve after he's come all this way.

Scrimshaw keeps staring at me and I shift my weight from one foot to the other, then back again. My bladder feels as full as a reservoir after a storm. I guess the morning's coffee and the water must add up to more than the gallons I've sweated out.

Scrimshaw says, "If you need to pee, just go behind a rock and pee. Nobody's gonna look." He turns his attention to selecting a chisel.

"No special place calling me to pee?"

"Just don't pee on any carvings."

I walk up the trail a short distance and duck behind a rock. I hope it's not a sacred rock and I hope it doesn't have its mouth open calling to some crazy artist. At least there are no carvings on it. I take my time and then stretch a bit and rotate my shoulders, sore after toting that tool bag. The sun is high in the sky. Between the early morning wake up, the hiking, and the heat, I'm feeling drowsy, and I've had just about enough. This was sort of interesting for a while, but it's getting old. As I stroll back, I concoct a plan to divert us to the car for another water bottle and from there try to convince everyone to go home.

Scrimshaw has carved two large, intricate figures above the trail, a coyote and a cloud, and two stick-figure people that look caveman compared to the rest of his work. "You're fast," I remark.

"When the rock speaks to you and is in harmony with your mind, hands, and soul, there's no hesitation." Scrimshaw grabs a rasp and adds texture to the cloud. "Rain cloud," Scrimshaw says. "A sign of change." He points to the other large figure. "Coyote. The trickster. The shape shifter. The transformer."

"That's nice." I look around. "Hey, where's Etcher?" A bunch of his tools litter the ground near his bag. "He go to water the rocks too?"

Scrimshaw keeps adding details and texture to the carving before eventually replying, "He had to go."

"What do you mean, go?"

Scrimshaw shrugs. "Go."

"Go where? He's not leaving without us, is he?" I squat next to Scrimshaw.

"No, he can't do that." Scrimshaw looks at me, then goes back to working the rock. "I got the key, anyway. But even if your friend had the key, he couldn't go."

"What do you mean?"

"He's in the Outback now."

My eyes narrow. "You mean he wandered around and got lost? If he's lost out here, we need to look for him, or go and get help."

"Oh, he doesn't need that." Scrimshaw stops work and surveys the new carving.

I look too. A cold, cold chill washes over my body. The sun's still beating down hot as sin, yet goose bumps break out all over. In the carving, the representation of the rock that Scrimshaw is actually working on has a smaller version of the same carving. And the rock within that carving seems to have a smaller version…and then I notice that one of the stick figures carved into the rock is waving. Frantically. For the first time, I see it has a man bun. Was that there when I came back from peeing? The chill turns to ice.

I look slowly at Scrimshaw and rise to my feet. My head feels light but my body feels heavy. "That…that stick figure…that's not Etcher. It can't be. It isn't possible."

"To you, no." Scrimshaw stands up and faces me. "Don't worry, he'll settle down. He hasn't adjusted to Rock Time yet. He'll stop wiggling soon."

My tongue feels thick and dry. The sun's glare is unbearably harsh. A wave of numbness washes over me; my legs feel foreign, rubbery. I sway and Scrimshaw puts his hands on my shoulders to steady me, his face close to mine, his eyes piercing, angry. I fumble for words and finally rattle in a strained whisper, "What the hell is going on?"

"I told you things happen in the Outback that you wouldn't believe. And surprise, surprise, you didn't believe. Now maybe you believe."

I nod. How can I not believe? I don't know how or why, but I know that stick figure impossibly waving in the rock is somehow Etcher. "Please, Scrimshaw, we get it. Please, let Etcher out of there. Please!"

Scrimshaw shakes his head. "Can't do that, it's too late for that. Too late for him. Too late for you." His grip on my shoulders tightens. Our eyes meet, his pupils large and black and infinitely deep, a distinct universe bordered by his white bandana and the brim of his brown hat. I can't move, can't look away, can't stop feeling walls that aren't there closing in.

Some part of me understands that the second stick figure carved into the rock is for me. The walls that aren't there is the rock itself closing in around me, trying to trap me like a fly in amber. I close my eyes. It's Scrimshaw; Scrimshaw is trying to force me into the rock. How can he do that? How can this happen? This is wrong!

A ball of fury forms in the pit of my stomach and radiates outward. What is this artsy-fartsy bullshit? This can't be happening and I can't let it happen. I open my eyes wide and clasp my hands on Scrimshaw's shoulders, rage pulsing from the core of my being with a viciousness I never knew was in me. I squeeze Scrimshaw's shoulders hard and his grip on mine loosens. I throw my head back, open my mouth, and start to scream, louder and louder as I grip tighter and tighter. Every muscle tenses until my whole body is quivering. The walls stop closing in, waver like

ORIGINATION

heat mirages. My scream of effort turns to a scream of triumph as the walls explode outward from my psyche, ejected like the body rejecting poison in a long, voluminous river of paranormal projectile vomit.

I stop screaming, and gradually, I stop shaking. I'm alone. Sort of. I'm still standing on the ridge. There are still two stick figures carved into the rock. The one with the man bun isn't moving anymore. The one with the domed hat with feathers is moving, though. It's moving a lot.

I take a deep breath and a long exhale. Etcher *and* Scrimshaw are trapped in the rock. Scrimshaw's stick figure moves ever more slowly, as if through water, then molasses, then tar. What is it with me and artists? I wanted to escape this…this…whatever is happening around me, but instead, I brought it with me. And now Etcher is…Etcher is…I don't know what Etcher is.

Stick Figure Scrimshaw has stopped moving.

How can I get Etcher out of there? I try to focus on the unseen walls, but they're not there and imagining them doesn't make it happen. I close my eyes and visualize a vortex pulling Etcher out of the stone. Whatever is inside of me that turned the tables on Scrimshaw isn't there anymore. Was it ever there, in me? Or did something go wrong and boomerang on Scrimshaw?

"Abracadabra," I say lamely. There's no magic word or magic wand or magic amulet. There's no damn magic at all now that Scrimshaw's gone. And Etcher is gone. Gone like my other artist friends. I stare at the carving, at the two still stick figures that show no sign of life. Maybe they're on Rock Time. Maybe they're alive in there and maybe they'll get out someday. But not today.

I become aware of the sun again, somehow dead overhead already and frying my neck to what will be a crispy glowing red. I'm bathed in sweat. How long have I been staring at the carving? I lick my dry lips with a tongue fuzzy from dehydration. I can't stay here, but how can I leave? I stare at the carving. It offers no answers.

I lick my lips again, then bend down, gather Etcher's tools, and place them in his bag. I have no idea what I'll tell Etcher's parents, but they should have his carving tools. Maybe the easiest thing would be to mail 'em to them anonymously and lay low for a while. Maybe move to another town, another state, another country, maybe swear off having artist friends.

I shoulder the bag, then dig the car key fob out of Scrimshaw's backpack. I look at the rock, hoping the figures will start moving and then emerge and be people again. They don't.

"See you, Etcher. If I can ever figure out how to get you out of there, I'll be back." I start down the ridge trail toward the car, then stop and walk back to the carving. I frown at Stick Figure Scrimshaw. "I guess it's like you said; Rock Time does move fast sometimes. Faster than even you would believe. I guess you didn't understand that any better than I did." I turn and hike down the trail.

ORIGINATION

S.L. LEITNER

Life During Collegetime

> *Why stay in college? Why go to night school?*
> *Gonna be different this time*
> *Can't write a letter, can't send no postcard*
> *I ain't got time for that now*
>   *—The Talking Heads, Life During Wartime*

Sometimes life in college seems like life during wartime. Pop quizzes going off like landmines, questions from pretentious professors firing like live bullets, finals dropping like hydrogen bombs, and no cover to be found. This combo of constant assaults on student warriors' nerves saddles them with a braincase of anxio-intellectual PTSD. In these stories, the students fight back.

- *Every Mad Dog Has His Day*
  Who the dummy is, is entirely unclear.
- *The Great Cafeteria Food Fight and Ice Cream Raid of 1981*
  Who the dummies are, is entirely clear.

S.L. LEITNER

Every Mad Dog Has His Day

Late one night, Mad Dog burst into our dorm room and declared, "Johnson, tonight we're going hunting."

"For what? I ain't got a gun."

"Neither have I, but we're still going hunting. Come on." Mad Dog strode out the door, my unfinished homework fluttering in his wake. I carefully weighed the academic merits and potential lifelong benefits derived from building good habits of hard, fruitful labor uninterrupted by frivolous distraction, versus the uncertain fate of joining Mad Dog in his daily dose of surreality.

I tried not to step on the homework papers as I grabbed my jacket and trotted out the door. I caught up to him at Agent Orange, my decrepit Datsun 510 station wagon. "Come on, *Ternbull*," he taunted at my tardiness. He knew how much I hated my last name.

"It's *Johnson*," I reminded him, forgetting to unlock the passenger door as I cranked up and took off, accompanied by Mad Dog's gratifying serenade of profanity. I stopped two blocks later. After a few false starts, I let him in. "Where we going, now?"

"Up to Oroville, *Johnson*." His voice tweaked as he grinned his wide grin full of white white teeth and stared his wide-eyed stare with glistening black pupils.

Just after Yuba City, Mad Dog started rolling joints with wild abandon. He had a new pack of Zig Zags and he needed them all. In his zeal, Mad Dog shredded most of the papers just before he could lick the gum, causing a downpour of pot all over his lap. The two joints that survived the massacre looked like saplings after a hurricane.

"There!" he exclaimed proudly, as if he had twisted a feat of engineering genius.

"We got any beer?" I asked, accelerating to all of the fifty-five miles an hour that Agent Orange's fuel-rejection engine could muster.

"Slow down! We're almost here." Mad Dog tried to light one of the saplings. "Turn left there," he said, waving vaguely between puffs. A minute later he wheezed, "Ere," and passed me the joint. It had a run that spiraled uniquely around its bumps, clumps, and twists. It looked a bit like a witch's warty hooked nose and smelled like dung.

"Whoops," I said, accidentally flinging the pathetic thing out the window. "Sorry. That was clumsy of me."

I expected some sort of rebuke, but instead Mad Dog grabbed my shoulder and shouted, "Hey! Turn right here!"

The fluorescent orange butt of my station wagon skidded halfway through the intersection on its bald, underinflated tires. "Before the next turn, don't give me so much advance warning," I said and shot him an unnoticed glare.

"The place is right over there." Mad Dog pointed through a chain-link fence at a huge field of grass strewn with shadowy objects. In the near corner an oval running track surrounded an area with long-jump pits, two high jumps, and bars for pull-ups. In the distance a few dim bulbs barely revealed three low, plain buildings. "Pull over on the shoulder and park."

"Now what?"

"Now we're going hunting."

Mad Dog catapulted out of the car, raced across the street and jumped the fence before I could shut off the headlights and lock up. A moment later I joined him and we sped out onto the grass. First we came across a sort of jungle gym. I knew we'd never fit that into Agent Orange.

Next we discovered a mini workout area, with a slanted bench for sit ups and logs cut to different heights for step exercises. I asked Mad Dog, "What is this place? An Olympic training center?"

"It's spy training camp, *Johnson*." He laughed. "It's the fireman's training center or something like that. It's been around for a long time."

"Are there still any firemen here?"

"Sure." He tromped off into the grass searching for plunder. "But they're all asleep right now. They had a hard day of training and wouldn't wake up if we dynamited their dorm."

"I hope you're right."

Mad Dog suddenly broke into a run. He stopped by a dark lump lying prostrate in the grass and yelped, "I found it!"

"Well keep a bit quieter about it! It doesn't look like it's going anywhere." I caught up and stared at the lump. "What, finally found your intellectual equal?"

"It's a fireman's dummy!" Mad Dog left his jaw hanging open as he grinned.

"So?"

"Don'tcha get it? Don't you know what this means?"

"I already said, it means you finally found your intell—"

"Where's your imagination!"

"I keep it locked up in a Mason jar in our room so it doesn't get in the way of my studies."

Mad Dog clutched his head for a moment, then said in an agonized whine, "This is the *prize*. This is the buck with the most points, the biggest fish, the toppest ramen. The fun we can have with this is endless!"

I shrugged, then bent to lift the thing by the shoulders. Unfortunately, somebody had nailed it to the ground.

"It's filled with lead pellets," Mad Dog explained. "It weighs about a hundred and eighty pounds. And it's highly uncooperative." He grinned his crazy, happy grin, as if "highly uncooperative" were a desirable trait.

Mad Dog occasionally has a talent for understatement. Not only was the pellet-filled dummy uncooperative, it was downright ornery. Its limbs insisted on flopping along and strictly obeying the laws of gravity, beating us about the neck and shoulders.

"Are you sure this thing only weighs a hundred and eighty pounds? It feels more like a hundred and eighty thousand."

Mad Dog grunted. "Maybe it is. I was never good with numbers."

Through a veil of sweat I saw Agent Orange, only a few million miles away. "What are we going to do with this monster, anyway? We don't need anyone else to use the carpool lane."

"This lovely creature will make for a killer spring quarter, Johnson. Don't underestimate it."

After a few minutes of lugging the dummy, scenes of the Spanish Inquisition were floating before my eyes. I could see prisoners flayed by nine-tailed whips with metal studs, prisoners with hands thrust into molten lead, prisoners impaled on long, sharp spikes; I was jealous of the light punishment they were getting. My lovely station wagon seemed no closer even though we kept staggering toward it. "I thought you said the *fun* we could have with this was endless, not the torture."

"Shut up and keep moving, Johnson."

We finally dragged that horrible thing all the way to the fence, not kicking, not screaming, but being one hell of a bitch anyway. When we dropped the load to catch a breath, I expected dawn to break any minute.

The fence was only a bit taller than me and had been easy to hop on the way in. Now it looked like Fenway's Green Monster. I couldn't imagine hoisting the dummy, which had somehow turned into a hippo shortly after we picked it up, above our heads to get it over that fence.

I looked at Mad Dog. "How about if I jump the fence and you chuck the dummy over. I'll catch him," I offered.

"Come on," Mad Dog coaxed, "it's not far now. Just over the fence and across the street, then it's all easy from there." We hoisted the dummy to our shoulders, then lifted mightily with grunting snorts like twin mustangs. A moment later the dummy was on the ground by the fence. Unfortunately, it was on top of us and we were still on the wrong side of the fence.

Dawn really was breaking by the time we figured out how to liberate the dummy. We propped it up against the fence and lifted it until we could hook its arms over the top. Next, we each grabbed one leg, just above the knee. With a "One, two, THREE!" we lifted the thing up and heaved with the last bit of stubbornness in our protesting bodies. The dummy's raised arms, head and shoulders cleared the fence with ease. Its torso caught on the top of the chain links and started to scrape back. Mad Dog had the presence of mind to grab both legs and give an upward thrust, juggling the fickle momentum from backward to forward. Leaving only a minimal layer

ORIGINATION

of its peach-colored plastic skin on the fence, it took a header into the dirt on the other side.

We hauled ourselves over the fence and dragged the dummy partway into the road before I let go.

Mad Dog looked at the dummy, then at me, then back at the dummy.

"I ain't gonna carry it no more," I declared.

"Why?"

I walked to Agent Orange.

"Come on, man, it's just across the street," Mad Dog pleaded. "You dragged it this far."

"Yeah, and I've had enough." I unlocked the door, got in, and cranked it up. Mad Dog just stood there in the first light, hanging on to the dummy's arms and staring at me, looking like somebody who's just been told he has twenty-four hours to live.

I pulled out and circled the wagon until the back hatch was in front of Mad Dog and the dummy. Mad Dog's crazy, happy grin returned. "I knew I could count on you, *Johnson*."

A minute later, Agent Orange's four-hamster-power engine had us heading home at the breathtaking speed of almost 50 miles per hour. "I wasn't sure we were going to be able to do it," Mad Dog said. "That fence almost ruined my day."

"But it didn't."

Mad Dog grinned. "I guess every Mad Dog has his day."

S.L. LEITNER

The Great Cafeteria Food Fight and Ice Cream Raid of 1981

Many people who have eaten in a school cafeteria dream about taking part in a food fight. This primal Jungian dream started long before John Belushi's famous food fight in the movie *Animal House*. It began with an anonymous but blessed person, who, with nose tightly pinched, noticed the origins of their lunch were harder to identify than month-old roadkill and the consistency of what was trying to pass as food vacillated between goop and gristle.

I was fortunate enough to live the dream. I not only participated in a food fight, better still, I instigated it. Best of all, none of us got caught. And nobody who wasn't in on the plan ever knew the truth of the matter, not until now, anyway.

The cafeteria served three off-campus dorms; two nice, modern, large ones called Eliot and Dickinson, and one small, shabby, ancient one called Longfellow. I lived in the two-story tar-topped disaster that was Longfellow along with 24 other men, and I use the term about as loosely as possible, and 25 women. The men were all on the ground floor and the women were all on the top floor.

And we had one Resident Advisor.

The RA was supposed to keep the students in line and prevent them from wrecking the place. When I moved into Longfellow, I arrived early and the place seemed empty. I wandered down the corridor on the men's floor, marveling at the chipped paint, torn carpeting, and burned out light bulbs of my first home away from home. I heard my favorite band, Pink Floyd. It was Dark Side of the Moon, sounding great even through a door. Something smelled pretty good even through that door, too.

I knocked.

"It's open."

I entered into a cloud of smoke and a bong thrust in my direction. A few other early arrivals sat on the floor or perched on the bed. The mustachioed blonde guy thrusting the bong at me sat in the only chair. A reel-to-reel and mid-size Advent speakers occupied most of the desk.

"That sounds great!" I said, accepting the bong and a lighter.

"Six hours, nothing but Floyd," said mustachioed blonde guy. "I'm Fifer, your RA."

⌛ ⌛ ⌛ ⌛ ⌛

In contrast to Longfellow's 50 residents, Eliot housed 700 students and Dickinson housed 370. Eliot and Dickinson had swimming pools, hot tubs, gyms, and spacious apartment-style rooms with kitchenettes and private bathrooms.

Longfellow featured a parking lot covered with loose gravel. Every time a car drove through it, shrapnel spit against the room walls in an annoying aural tap dance. Longfellow's single-room caves featured two narrow beds, built-in wooden structures that almost mimicked desks but which may have been intended as dressers, one closet that fit two people's clothes about as comfortably as a onesie fit an elephant, and pre-stained, paper-thin, puke-green carpeting.

Instead of a convenient, private lavatory in each room, each floor had a communal bathroom. I can't speak for the ladies room, but the bathroom on the men's floor was only a slight improvement on an open pit in that it was a covered pit.

The walls between the cells that passed as rooms were educationally instructive in that they really brought home the mathematical concept of an infinitely thin two-dimensional plane. If someone in a room farted, the walls vibrated like audio speakers and amplified the sound in the adjoining rooms with the power of an electric bass guitar. On nights when the cafeteria served baked beans, the dorm sounded like John Entwhistle on steroids.

We Longfellows responded to these differences in accommodations by banding together in a confederation of misfits, stoners, pre-med students, and outlaws. All of us were admitted too late to find a decent place to stay and assignment to Longfellow was our just and inequitable punishment.

We tolerated the run-down conditions at Longfellow by taking a perverse pride in our fortitude. The common disaster of our dilapidated dorm knit us together as a merry band of degenerates combined with a few serious students, each subgroup affecting the other and opening its doors of perception a crack wider. I myself clocked a full seven hours, thirteen minutes, and forty-three seconds of study time during the first quarter alone, probably tripling the total study time across my entire high school career.

For a while, things ran as smoothly as they could. And at least we received the same cafeteria and food privileges as the tenants of the two larger dorms, so we were all being punished equally.

And then came the day they took even that away from us.

The administrators announced each dorm would be allowed to host an ice cream social. The cafeteria would provide five-gallon tubs of ice cream for the occasion. Not tub—tubs! The residents of each dorm feverishly began to plan ice cream socials, each trying to find a theme that would blow the other dorms away. As plans developed, the administrators visited each dorm to ensure that its party would have an acceptable theme.

Longfellow had chosen its most photogenic residents to present the case for a toga party themed ice cream social in the best worst tradition of every bad college satire. Some of us uglier types hung around the fringes, ready to coach the team if necessary and cheer our success. Our RA, Fifer, was there to back us up with all the gravitas of a pre-med student about to ruin the next ten years of his life with grad school and medical internships, and then ruin the following twenty years trying to pay back the crushing student loan debt.

We had prepared rigorously, bringing together the mighty powers of Jack Daniels, Johnny Walker, and Humboldt's Finest to concoct our grand plan. Our arrows of rhetorical logic were notched in the bowstring of persuasive debate, but we never got a chance to pull back and release those arrows and pierce those administrators in their empty, heartless chests. Before our lead presenter could speak, the chief administrator said, "I know you've all worked hard to come up with a theme, but since your dorm is only fifty people, we can't justify having a party just for you." As we gasped and cried out in dismay, he continued, "You can go to Eliot's or Dickinson's ice cream social instead."

"They can come to ours!" we shouted. "We're as good as they are! We pay the same for our hovels as they pay for their mansions! It's only fair to let us host an ice cream social too—we can all go to each other's!"

But our arguments fell on deliberately deaf ears. The pompous pimply-ass administrators had made up their minds and Longfellow was left out in the cold again. The administrators departed and we stood silent, the wind properly taken from our once-billowing sails. As a few dejected residents trickled out, Baydger said, "We shouldn't have to take this."

"We sure as hell shouldn't," several of us grumbled in agreement.

"We can't let them get away with it," Baydger said. "We have to do something."

We agreed amen to that, but what to do? Then my roommate, Preacher's Boy, said, "There's only one way this can go. We gotta get the ice cream."

"How?" said Walker, whose practicality streak only asserted itself at inconvenient moments such as when everyone was het up for action but nobody knew what to do. We stood in silence, rubbing our chins and crossing our arms and looking at our shoes, hoping someone else would come up with something.

"Let's look at this like a chess game," I finally said. "Except our objective isn't checkmate, it's get the ice cream. So the first thing is, where's the ice cream?" I raised an eyebrow. "It's in the Dining Commons, in big, convenient, five-gallon tubs."

"So it is, so it is," said Baydger, "but what does that buy us? The Dining Commons is locked up when it's closed. And when it's open, there are two RAs at the door checking everything. And that's the only way in or out unless you're severely overcooked spinach or severely undercooked chicken, then you go out in someone's stomach—but not for long, of course." We all gave a perfunctory chuckle for the barf joke. "Even if we could grab a tub, we couldn't get it out of there."

Hollow Legs Lisa tossed down a shot of Cuervo and then said, "How about when the Dining Commons is closed?"

"Of course!" Mad Dog yelled. "We wait until three in the morning, smash a window, grab the ice cream, and everything's copacetic."

"Smash a window?" said Walker. "That won't set off any alarms or wake anybody up."

"But before anyone gets there, we'll be gone," Mad Dog argued.

"After anyone gets there, we get kicked out of school."

"We're not breaking into the Dining Commons," I said. "We have to do this in broad daylight, when it's open." I looked around the room. "Chess strategy and tactics: what's standing in the way of us doing that and how do we beat it?"

"The Dining Commons is always full of people, they'd all see us, duh," said Hollow Legs.

"There are two RAs at the door—we'd never get past them," said Baydger. "Duh," he added, nodding at Hollow Legs.

"Hmmm. You know," Walker said, "Fifer's an RA."

Fifer looked at Walker. "Yeah. And you're an alcoholic. So what?"

"You have door duty at the Dining Commons sometimes, right?"

"Yeah, I take my turn like all the RAs. But like Baydger said, there are two of us. We'd have to bribe the other RA."

I grinned. It was an evil grin. Being evil in righteous indignant vengeance is fun. "Not necessarily, boys and girls. I think I have an idea, but it'll take all of us to do it, the whole dorm. And you're the key, Fifer." We adjourned to Fifer's tiny room—the only single-person room in the dorm—and gathered around his reel-to-reel player with Pink Floyd playing softly in the background and a bong bubbling softly in the foreground. The dorm's usual suspects were there: Preacher Boy, Baydger, Mad Dog, Walker, me; Sharon and Hollow Legs Lisa represented the women on the upstairs floor. We barely had enough space to pass the bong around.

"OK bright boy, whatcha got?" asked Walker.

"We play it like magicians," I said.

"I thought we were playing chess," Preacher's Boy cut in.

"We're doing both at the same time and that's how we're going to win."

I paused to hoof down a hit for emphasis. "For the magic, we get 'em to watch one hand while the other hand steals all the ice cream," I wheezed through a cloud of exhaled smoke. "And here's the chess part: we don't just take one five-gallon drum, we take *all* the ice cream. Checkmate."

Walker's eyes narrowed. "Are you saying that in broad daylight, we just walk in, wave a hand, and walk out with four five-gallon drums of ice cream? Just like that?"

"Exactly," I said, rather pleased with myself. "Well, sort of exactly. The broad daylight part of it is right, anyway."

"So, what..." mused Walker, "...we disguise the ice cream drums as students?" Most of us giggled.

"Nope. We just march 'em right out the door. Which Fifer will be guarding."

"So will another RA," said Fifer.

"Yes and no," I replied. "The other RA's gonna be busy at the time. Really busy. Because we're going to see to it that he's busy. At least, Squad One will."

"Squad One?" asked Walker. "What's Squad One?"

"So glad you asked." I passed the empty bong to Preacher's Boy and leaned into the group. "We're going to split up into three squads. Each squad's going to have a leader." I glanced around the circle and briefly looked each person in the eye. "And everyone in each squad will know exactly what their job is." I let my gaze settle on one person. "Especially you, Fifer."

"Especially me?" Fifer asked. "Which squad will I lead?"

"Your own special squad of one. So it's really four squads."

"Wait a minute, you say we need fifty people to do this?" Walker asked.

"Fifty-one—twenty-five guys, twenty-five girls, one RA. We all earn the ice cream, we all share the ice cream. One for Longfellow and Longfellow for all."

"My long fellow's only for some, not for all," Walker said.

"Ah, the obligatory dick joke, no better way to start off." I smiled at the group. "This is what I was thinking..."

ORIGINATION

Our Dining Commons was a rectangular, one-story building whose walls were mostly windows, maybe so diners could see out, but more likely to warn prospective diners about the day's menu. Its single entrance, near one of the corners, was also its single exit.

The first thing you saw on the way in and the last thing you saw on the way out was the ice cream. Each of two rectangular freezers against the wall contained two glorious five-gallon tubs of delectable brain freeze. The location provided strong incentive for diners to leave when they were done with the main meal and make room for more diners.

Fifteen rows of tables occupied the main part of the Dining Commons. Each row had two long, narrow tables, and each table seated a couple dozen diners. Food stations flanked the tables on three sides, with the entrance and the ice cream tubs we craved on the fourth side.

We timed our entry carefully so the place was still packed with residents, but not so packed that we wouldn't be able, with a little work, to claim a squad's worth of space at a table. Fifer and another RA manned the only door and checked everyone's residency ID as they entered.

My squad entered the Dining Commons en masse, which was normal for our group of misfits. We usually commandeered a table or two and ate together, separate from the privileged scions of Eliot and Dickinson. Three of us started saving spaces at a table near the middle of the dining area while the rest of us bellied up to the various food dispensing areas. I opted for a late breakfast and got eggs over easy. Over very easy. Fifteen seconds on side one, ten seconds on side two. The cooks gave me funny looks and asked me a few times if I was sure before they shook their heads and cooked the eggs, or at least imparted a tiny bit of heat to them. They came out perfect—egg yolks barely warm, whites barely cooked enough to sort of hold together. I added some potatoes with extra grease—that's the only way they were served—and some cottage cheese, and then made my way to our table.

As my squad filled their plates, they began to assemble at the table, politely asking others to move so that the little band of miscreants from Longfellow could sit together as usual. I nodded with approval at a plate with a Sloppy Joe that made normal Sloppy Joes look seriously buttoned-down, a plate with a salad swimming in what looked like Ranch, Russian, *and* Blue Cheese dressing, and a bowl of chili with shredded cheese food substitute melted into it and a runny excuse for sour cream sloshing on top.

We waited politely for the rest of the squad to load their plates and join us. As the last few stragglers seated themselves, the other two squads entered the Dining Commons, broken up into smaller groups. They found seats near the entrance or milled around the end of the salad bar near the entrance.

I looked around the table, nodding slowly and catching eyes to let everyone know that it was time. I took a spoon and balanced a warm, liquid bundle of over-exceptionally-easy egg on it. Holding the handle firmly in my left hand with the head of the spoon pointing in front of me, I bent the head of the spoon down with my right hand and then let go without aiming. The payload arced back over my shoulder and landed on a poor, anonymous victim.

Every fight has innocent casualties and this fight would be no different. Several others in my squad took their chili, their gravy-laden mashed potatoes, their yogurt, and their diced tomatoes, and did the same, carefully maintaining casual conversation and never looking to see who got hit.

It only took a few launches before muttered, "What the hells," from ordinary students gave way to the first genuine roar of indignation. The victim was a football-player-looking jock dude with a chest like a gorilla. The jock dude looked around. It was critical that none of our team looked at him as he scanned the room. We knew that some innocent—well, potentially innocent, it's good to keep an open mind—person would have witnessed the splat or the aftermath and be laughing. Jock Dude found an innocent laugher and threw a handful of stew at him. Instead of his intended target, he hit another jock dude and his girlfriend.

Jock Dude Two stood up, yelled, "You asshole!," and heaved his half-eaten burger at Jock Dude One. He missed, but connected with another potentially innocent victim. Innocence went out the window along with decorum and nature took its course. The air began to fill with errant, goopy missiles. I gave the signal and my squad rose as one and headed for the exit as the artillery fire heated up. The last member of my squad to march out of the Dining Commons, Hollow Legs Lisa, casually remarked to the RAs at the door, "Hey, what's going on in there?"

"What do you mean?" said the RA who wasn't Fifer, as Hollow Legs sashayed away. The RAs looked at each other and then looked in the window. Food seemed to be everywhere except on plates and was getting more everywhere every moment. The RA who wasn't Fifer turned to Fifer and said, "What do we do? Everyone in the place is throwing food!" He gestured toward the dining room. "Should we call someone? What should we do?"

Fifer shrugged. "I dunno. I guess we should go in and stop it?"

The other RA said, "One of us has to stay and guard the door." He straightened his shoulders, pursed his lips, and then said, "I'll stop the fight." Fifer could have sworn the other RA's face turned slightly up in a futile attempt to look heroic. "You make sure nobody gets out."

Before Fifer could reply, the other RA yanked open the door and rushed into the Dining Commons, yelling, "That's enough!" as he ran.

Fifer shook his head and grinned. "And I had all these great reasons why he should go in instead of me." The entrance of the RA who was not Fifer signaled the other two squads to leap into action.

Squad Two lined up and formed a human wall, hiding the ice cream coolers from the rest of the room, not that anyone was looking. Everyone was either hucking food at each other or hiding under a table.

Squad Three ducked in behind Squad Two's human wall, bent over halfway so nobody could see them, and made for the door, grabbing the four five-gallon tubs of ice cream on the way. Fifer let them out, followed by the human shield squad. Then Fifer locked the door and watched the other RA get buried in creamed corn and the soup of the day as he struggled to stop the food fight.

⏳ ⏳ ⏳ ⏳ ⏳

Back at the dorm, all fifty of us waited for Fifer to return before we dug into the ice cream. It took him a while. When he returned to our pantheon of questions that all amounted to "Did we get caught?", he had a strange little smile playing about his lips.

"No, they uh, they uh, they...actually, they're giving us a commendation."

"For what? Best of use of cafeteria food?" Walker quipped.

Fifer ignored him. "They checked the IDs of everyone in the Dining Commons, and guess what? Nobody from Longfellow, only residents of Eliot and Dickinson. So we're the good kids now."

He paused while we hooted, laughed, and started serving the ice cream.

"Oh, one more thing," said Fifer. "Because we were the only dorm that wasn't involved in the food fight, they're rewarding us by giving us our own ice cream social."

ORIGINATION

S.L. LEITNER

What I Talk About When I Talk About God

Musical references title the previous three sections. For this section, I chose a reference to one of my eight favorite authors, Haruki Murakami, and his book *What I Talk About When I Talk About Running*.

Some religions say we are made in God's image. If that's true, then if I look hard enough, I should be able to see some trace of God in me. I have a sense of humor, or at least an attempted sense of humor. When I look in the mirror every morning, my image gives me the feeling that God must have a sense of humor too.

When Mr. Murakami wrote *What I Talk About When I Talk About Running*, he talked about much more than running. In *What I Talk About When I Talk About God*, I talk about much more than God. In Mr. Murakami's book, running is a gateway to other concepts. In this section of the book, other concepts are a gateway to God.

God can be a touchy subject, so may I finish by saying, please don't hit me.

- *The Irate Businessman*
  A businessman struggles to resurrect a struggling business.
- *I Am*
  Time machines aren't supposed to work. At least, not *this* way.
- *The Gardener*
  The Aristocrats are bored and everybody better duck.

S.L. LEITNER

The Irate Businessman

Jehovah plodded to the plain white videophone. He stared at the blank screen and tugged absently at his flowing white beard. He sucked in his gut and mumbled, "Get me the District Supervisor." After two beeps, the screen flashed on.

"Pardon me, District Supervisor. This is Jehovah, District God of Earth."

"Earth?" Bushy white eyebrows beetled. "Oh yes, Earth." He cleared his throat and took on a brisk, businesslike tone. "What's on your mind, Jevohah?"

"It's Jehovah, sir. We're having a small problem here." Jehovah resisted the urge to stare at his feet. "Or rather, a bit of a largish problem. The indigenous biogenerators are praying less frequently and less fervently than they did when we first wowed them with parting seas, walking on water, and that sort of thing. Many have lost faith, some without even realizing it. Even those who still subscribe are dissident, squabbling amongst themselves over petty details in our major brochure, the Bible—"

"Are you suggesting that sending Christ wasn't good enough for them? He's our top strategist and closer."

"That was about two thousand planetary revolutions around their sun—they call them years—ago. Since they only live about seventy-five or eighty years apiece, the species memory gets muddled pretty fast. After Christ made his pitch, we were doing a good job taking market share from the Olympians and some smaller companies that were trying the polytheistic route, but then everything changed.

"A rival company sent a sales rep called Muhammad. This Muhammad guy piggybacked on what we did and took away a *considerable* portion of our potential business. It was really unfair business tactics to offer all those virgins for martyrs, genius though it was. And it cut us off from expanding the business in some areas. The indigenous biogenerators—"

"Just say subscribers," the District Supervisor cut in, "we don't have to be technical."

"Fine, the subscribers have also split our product into a number of rival offshoots because of quibbles over the marketing department's phrasing of the Bible." Jehovah scratched his beard, then began twiddling a finger through it, shrouding the finger in a white spiral of hair. "One group still follows the paths our first project set up when we sent those memos to that Moses fellow. Marketing should put out one definitive, clearly written document that doesn't confuse the biogenerators. Er, subscribers."

"That would be a major project and it's not in the budget," said the District Supervisor. "From what you've said, we need to restore the subscribers' faith to at least regain the market share we've lost."

"Yes," Jehovah nodded vigorously, "that's the bottom line. We need to do something really miraculous, like making it rain gold dust or maybe refined oil."

"Hold on a minute," the District Supervisor said. He looked at the screen embedded in his desk and whispered a few commands. After a moment he shouted, "Why didn't you tell me the prayer power reservoir for Earth was down to twenty percent?"

"I've been putting it in my reports since the prayer power reservoir dropped to eighty percent!"

"You know nobody reads the reports. You should have called me a long time ago. What am I supposed to tell the Regional Supervisor, eh?"

Jehovah untangled the finger corkscrewed into the depths of his beard with only minor uprooting of hair. "Tell him these subscribers need miracles. They need *something* to rekindle their faith so they'll start praying again and we can get the power reservoir up to acceptable levels."

ORIGINATION

The District Supervisor drummed his fingers on his desk, took a deep breath, and then let it out slowly. "You're sure a miracle will do the trick?"

Jehovah in turn took a deep breath, his hand white around the corporate Jesus-on-the-cross logo dangling from the chain around his neck, but the breath didn't want to come back out. Confrontations with the Super made him sweat and feel as if he had shown up at an important meeting in a transparent robe, and everyone could see his comfortable, but frilly, underwear. But the whole market was imploding; he had to do something.

The breath finally came back out. "I don't know what else to suggest, Supervisor. Greater numbers of potential subscribers are refusing to give their business to *any* company and just forgetting about the whole thing!"

"Why are they losing faith? Why aren't they praying anymore?"

"Unfortunately, they may be catching on."

"Catching on?"

"This is an unusual type of biopower source with an equally unusual subscription deal. Normally, we give biogeneration subscribers something of palpable value in return for their energy. For these subscribers, in return for expressing faith through prayer power, our brochure promises forgiveness, eternal happiness in Heaven, and an inner peace that eases their daily burdens. The marketing department was really pleased with themselves when they came up with that one."

"They should be," said the District Supervisor. "It's a brilliant plan and we've profited immensely from it."

"The problem is that we can't actually give them any of that. A number of subscribers give themselves some of that stuff—well, forgiveness and inner peace, anyway—and they usually credit us even though we had nothing to do with it. We've been harvesting their power for nothing more than the cost of maintenance." Jehovah shook his head. "Until now, anyway. Subscribers may have begun to realize we're not keeping up our end of the bargain."

"So you want to throw them a bone by giving them miracles?"

"If you have another idea, say it! Since we can't give them what sales and marketing promised, the only thing I can think of is to give them miracles. After all, it worked for Christ." Jehovah pursed his lips, then said, "We have to do something or we could lose this whole account."

"You make it sound even more serious than the numbers indicate."

"It is. The subscribers need miracles to confirm divine existence and they need them now!" Jehovah stamped his foot. "We need them now or we won't be able to provide the power our customers need. Our stock will plummet and then what will you tell the Regional Supervisor, and then what will he tell the VP, and then what will she tell the CEO, and then what will she tell the shareholders?"

The District Supervisor's eyes widened. He could have been on a golf course swallowing his pride and losing gracefully to his boss, the Regional Supervisor, or maybe to some bigwig from Buddha, Inc., or the Hinduism Conglomerate. Someone else could be sitting in his chair watching his career flash before his eyes. He wished the question *what could possibly be worse than throwing another game of golf to some bigshot* had not been answered with such stunning clarity.

Jehovah planted a hand on his hip, cleared his throat and glared at the screen. The District Supervisor shook himself out of his reverie and said, "All right, Jehovah, keep your shirt on. I'll tell you what we're gonna do. By we, I mean *you* of course . . ."

⧗ ⧗ ⧗ ⧗ ⧗

Schach Wilders propped himself against a wall of chipped stone and crumbling mortar in the shade of a burned out temple that once traded in salvation but now only peddled "miraculously delicious" Baklava. His girlfriend, Pandora, had conned Schach into making the sticky pilgrimage from the cool Berkeley hills to the sweltering middle eastern desert by threatening to take his credit cards on a week-long shopping frenzy at every mall in a 50-mile radius. A quick back-of-the-envelope calculation convinced Schach that the trip would be cheaper. A lot cheaper.

Schach wiped the length of his bony arm across his narrow forehead, wondering whether more dirt and sweat had gone from his forehead to his arm or vice-versa. All Schach could think about was getting something to drink, preferably a half-frozen oil can of Australian beer.

Fortunately, the bar area of Jerusalem had grown to the same proportions as the temple area, and was twice as gaudy and four times as popular. Schach and Pandora stopped in front of the largest establishment. It boasted a huge, pink-domed roof with a pastel-green crescent at its apex. A neon marquis surrounded by backlit plastic rocks proclaimed: *THE CRESCENT BAR—A RELIGIOUS EXPERIENCE*. Next to it rested a smaller, crooked sign that read:

This Prophecy Is Always True!

Happy Hour 5-7

Marvel at the Incredible **Jesusina**
and her *Magic Shroud Dance*

Cash Only!!

A long line of disheveled wayfarers filed in slowly, eager to pay any price for a cold drink.

Schach shrugged. "Well? Do we try this place or head for The Last Supper Bar and Grill over there?" He hooked his thumb toward what appeared to be an open-air bait shop in the mouth of an alley across the street. The proprietor passed his greasy hand over the fly-carpeted counter, and lo! What appeared but a variety of alluring sweetmeats and cakes! However, before the magic hand reached the counter's end, the flies had resettled and made the first half of the counter resume its disguise as a bait shop.

Pandora rolled her eyes. "You choose. You're the one who wants the damned drink in the first place."

"Don't say damned in a religious city, Pandy."

"Huh! *You* just said it."

Schach blinked reflexively as an immense puff of smoke rose from the alley. The Last Supper Bar and Grill had disappeared; not even a fly remained. Everyone stopped talking and gawked at the two men with long white beards and flowing white robes who had appeared in the middle of the alley. One coughed violently and the other held a large piece of paper.

"Oh goody!" Pandora shouted. "A street swami and his magic show. This is gonna be great, Schach!"

The one with the piece of paper turned it around and around with growing franticness. The other stopped coughing and Schach heard him wheeze *sotto voce*, "Let's stick to the blaze of glory and forget the smoke next time, whaddya say, huh Gabe?"

Gabriel nodded absently and then tried to fold up the large piece of paper. From his furrowed brow and clenched jaw, Schach guessed it wasn't folding back together the way it had unfolded. Pandora yelled, "Do a trick! Let's see some magic already!"

Gabriel looked startled. The other one whispered, "Just as Jehovah said. Why didn't you agree with him?"

"I didn't realize they were desperate." Gabriel squared his shoulders. "Let's get on with it and give 'em a few miracles."

Gabriel faced the people packing the entrance to the Crescent Bar. "Tell your brothers within that we have come to this holy place, the most populous temple in this blessed city—nowhere are prayers of thanks to God given so often and so fervently—to impart to you a message." He raised his voice. "Those of you waiting at the entrance to the temple, wait no longer, for it is not inside you must go."

From the front of the lined-up mob a Texan the size and approximate shagginess of a grizzly bear yelled, "The hell it's not! I'm gonna go in there and get me a drink! That is," he added sarcastically, "unless you can rustle me up a drink, Mr. Swami."

"Remove your hat," Gabriel instructed, "and hold it so the brim faces the heavens."

"Just what've you got in mind, stranger?" the Texan drawled, resting his meaty hands on his Michelin-man hips.

"You are thirsty," Gabriel answered. "I would give you drink."

The Texan grinned. "Awlright. Go ahead." He swept off his ten gallon hat and held it upside down. His grin disappeared and somehow reappeared on Gabriel's face. The Texan's eyes bulged and his face slowly turned from dough white to fire-ant red. Finally, he recovered his considerable voice and yelled, "What in the *HELL* do you think you're doing? You filled a two hunnerd n' fifty dollar hat full of God damned water! God damned water!" His body puffed up like a parade float. "You didn't even have the brains to make it whiskey!"

"Mayhaps you goofed," the other robed man said to Gabriel. "I think it's time to get to the big stuff—and the message the Super and Jehovah wrote up."

Gabriel nodded.

"Isn't it odd?" said Pandora. "These street swamis speak perfect English. I'm impressed!"

Schach glanced at the crowd. All eyes stared at the two white-robed men. "Y'know, Pandy, all these people are listening to these guys, but I know all these tourists aren't Americans and most of the street beggars can't speak much English. I wonder why they're listening."

"Look Schach, the talky one is raising his arms."

Gabriel said, "Behold," in a voice that echoed down the entire alley.

"Ooooh, that's a *good* trick!" Pandora gushed.

"He can do it because of the alley's shape," Schach explained with a knowing nod. "It's elementary acoustics."

Gabriel's voice boomed again. "I am the Archangel Gabriel."

To Schach's surprise, a portion of the crowd dropped to their knees in an attitude of prayer or prostration. Pandora giggled. A few tourists laughed. Schach decided that it was part of the act and laughed too.

Gabriel looked surprised and offended, but fixed his eyes on a spot on the Crescent Bar's grimy wall and continued in his echo-voice. "I *am* the Archangel Gabriel. I have come to prove God does indeed exist, and to show you His bounty with the first miracles in two thousand years."

The hulking Texan declared, "Your first God damned miracle better be gettin' me a new hat." He forsook his coveted place at the head of the line to stomp over and confront the two white-bearded interlopers.

Gabriel's eyes widened. "I beg your pardon!"

"You heard me, you connivin' little pile of prairie dog droppin's." The Texan shook a hairy paw under Gabriel's nose. "You ruined my hat, and you're gonna pay for it or I'm gonna knock your teeth out the other side of your tail."

Gabriel's lips twitched. "I am the Archangel Gabriel!" he insisted. "I have promised miracles, and miracles I shall perform." He started rolling back the right sleeve of his robe. "But first I'm going to—"

"Temper, Gabe," his companion chided, holding back Gabriel's arm.

Gabriel nodded, held his breath and counted to ten while the Texan scowled at him. He waved his hand. The Texan struggled vainly to resist the invisible pillow that pushed him back to the line. He tried to speak, but only a weak gurgle escaped his throat. Gabriel intoned, "It has come to our attention that the Muslims have blocked your Golden Gate. Our first miracle will be to open the gate. The Golden Gate," he raised his right hand dramatically, "will now unblock."

A group of Jerusalem natives cheered and ran to the city's sealed eastern gate, the famous Golden Gate. Pandora whined, "How did they know what he was talking about? He's speaking in English."

"It must be one of their tricks. They speak in several languages at once, but you only hear yours. I bet they'll have packed their bags and slinked out of town before those people get back."

Alas, the Golden Gate remained as plugged as someone on an all-cheese diet. However, for the first time in modern history at rush hour on a Monday morning, the traffic on San Francisco's equally famous Golden Gate Bridge mysteriously cleared up and flowed smoothly.

"For our next miracle," Gabriel continued, "the mighty temples of your false idols shall thunder to the ground in ruinous proclamation of their insignificance! Wherever men gather to worship false idols, destruction shall follow! It is done!"

The frenzied cheers cascading upon the head of the famous Spanish toreador Roberto Tasa de Calvados were followed by pieces of Barcelona's Plaza de Toros as the popular corrida collapsed around the startled fans, obliterating the object of their admiration.

On the other side of the world, with two down in the ninth, New York Yankees star centerfielder Jimmy "The Glove" Bonano settled under a fly ball to the roaring of 45,000 fans. He was rather annoyed to find three tons of stadium lights falling toward his mitt along with the baseball. *Somebody's gonna get whacked for this*, Jimmy thought. A second later, it turned out to be Jimmy.

Not being omniscient, Gabriel forged ahead. "These miracles we offer to you, God's children, to show you God has not forsaken you. Through the power of your prayer, He knows what trials and tribulations you endure, so pray fervently and often. Only through the miracle of prayer can the miracle of your desires be answered."

"Don't lay it on too thick," Gabriel's companion whispered.

"The numbers have dropped off drastically. They have to pray more often and with more feeling," Gabriel whispered back out the side of his mouth.

"Of course, of course." In a burst of well-intentioned inspiration, Gabriel's companion raised his hands and shouted, "Free miracles to the first ten prayers." Gabriel frowned. His companion shrugged and whispered, "Just a bit of creative incentive."

Gabriel's voice amplified to its echo proportions, drowning out the shouts of people hoping to get in one of the first ten prayers. "We will perform one final miracle before we leave." Slowly Gabriel raised both arms, squeezing every drop of anticipation from his audience. "Behold! Before you—"

A rumbling thunder of shouts from the alley's eastern end halted Gabriel's oration. Schach tried to peer over the crowd, but couldn't see anything. The cries grew louder. The crowd's eastern border swelled like a bubble and then burst as a swarm of outraged Jerusalemites broke through. The leader yelled something in Arabic or Yiddish or Hebrew or Sanskrit, Schach didn't know which, or maybe all of them were the same.

Gabriel looked at his partner in confusion as the wild-eyed mob surged forward and collapsed on them.

⌛   ⌛   ⌛   ⌛   ⌛

"Now what do you suggest?" the District Supervisor asked.

Jehovah's hand trembled as it tugged sharply on his beard, which had become over-tightly twiddled around his finger during the course of the conversation. He winced, not entirely from physical pain. "I don't think the damage is *irreparable*," he said, taking a step back and extricating his finger. "There must be a way to turn this to our advantage, or at least make our competition look bad."

"What do you have in mind?"

"Have in mind?" Jehovah echoed. "Well, er, ah, that is, the way I see it, you see . . . yes! Yes, of course, we have a problem with our knowledge of specific facts. The world down there has changed since our last visit. A lot." He gave a slight shake of his head. "In fact, the whole place has become rather complicated." Jehovah frowned. "When Gabe returned and found out about the bridge and all those other things, he was quite upset. He said our R&D people had to research miracles more thoroughly to take into account all of the new structures and customs."

"But he believes the subscribers want more miracles, in spite of the recent, ah, mishaps?"

"Oh yes. The first thing Gabe heard when he arrived was a woman screaming for magic. But they have to be the right sort of miracles and they must be properly executed."

"Hmmm. Put Gabe on the line."

"Right away." Jehovah stabbed the hold button to pause the transmission, dabbed his forehead with his sleeve, and then scuttled to an intercom on the opposite wall. He pushed the button and said, "Gabe, phone call."

"Just a minute," Gabriel replied in a grouchy tone.

"Now," Jehovah commanded firmly.

The Archangel Gabriel appeared with a pop of displaced air. A nasty purple bruise covered most of his forehead. One bloated lip shone pink and rubbery in tribute to a Jerusalemite's ring-laden knuckles. One hand pressed into a pulled muscle in the crook of his back. Jehovah shook his head and pretended to cough, but too late to hide his grin. He pointed at the phone and watched Gabriel limp to it. Gabriel pushed the hold button. The transmission resumed.

"This is the Archangel Gabriel."

"So you're convinced Earth needs miracles?"

"District Supervisor!" Gabriel's eyebrows shot up, compressing the bruise on his forehead and making him grimace. "Um, yes, yes I do. Subscribers were crying out for miracles. The first one I heard—"

"I know. But what miracles should we perform?"

"Product marketing is supposed to come up with answers to that question. I work in sales and presentation; I'm not even in marketing. I really don't know."

"I don't think marketing knows either," the District Supervisor mused.

"What we need is expert advice."

"Should we call in a consultant? Who could we get? Do you know any experts on Earth's inhabitants?"

A smile suffused the District Supervisor's face. He replied. "I know a whole *world* full of consultants. That woman who yelled for the miracle, for example. She must know what they want. Why not ask her?"

"Ask her?" Gabriel repeated.

"You've got the idea. Ask her. I believe it's called market research."

⧗ ⧗ ⧗ ⧗ ⧗

"Turn on the light, Schach."

Schach's eyes creaked open. He debated whether to groan out loud or curse in silence.

"The bed's too hard," Pandora whined. "And I thought I heard a noise. Turn on the light, Schach."

"All right," Schach mumbled, burrowing his head into his pillow.

"Scha-ach," Pandora bleated. "Schach!"

"All right!" Schach reached out to the bedside table and felt for the lamp. He found an overused tissue, a half-empty glass of water that was now completely empty, and a formerly dry paperback book.

After a moment, Schach resigned himself to sitting up and finding the switch. He slid up the headboard and clunked his head on the brass lamp holder sticking out of the wall. He cursed, eliciting a shocked, "Schach, we're in the holy city of Jerusalem!" from Pandora, and turned on the lamp. Schach glared at Pandora through eye slits the width of a wire and said, "There. Does the light make the bed any softer?"

"If the beds are anything like the ones in this city 2,000 years ago, flogging them for a fortnight with a meat tenderizer won't make them softer," said the Archangel Gabriel, who was sitting cross-legged at the foot of the bed.

"It's the street swami!" Pandora screeched, yanking the sheets up to cover herself. "How did you get in here?"

"I can go wherever I want." Gabriel raised his hand, palm toward

Pandora. "Don't be alarmed. I'm the Archangel Gabriel. I'm not here to hurt you, I'm one of the good guys. Sayyyy," he cocked his head and frowned. "You two aren't married, are you? Shouldn't you be in separate beds? Not to mention separate rooms?"

Schach and Pandora glanced at each other nervously. "They had one room left and it had only one bed," Schach lied.

Pandora added, "It's all completely innocent."

"All too tr—I mean perfectly true," Schach agreed ruefully. "Pandy gets these headaches—"

"Schach has back problems," Pandora cut in. "He can't sleep on the floor." She arched an eyebrow. "You wouldn't have a *lady* sleep on the floor, would you?"

"Uh, no, of course not," Gabriel replied. "Anyway, I'm here to—heyyyy, wait a minute. Then how come you're not wearing any—"

"What was it you were saying you were here for?" Pandora interrupted. "We had a long day sightseeing and shopping, and we'd like to get back to sleep if you don't mind. Maybe you could go and appear in someone else's room."

Gabriel waved his hands. "No, no, no. We need your help. When I appeared earlier and performed miracles, they went horribly awry. Well, maybe not *horribly*, I think that's a little harsh regardless of what the Super said, but I need to know what you people want in a miracle. If we do it right this time, it will confirm divine existence and people will once again turn to prayer."

Pandora's jaw unhinged slowly. "You want *me* to pick miracles for *you* to perform?"

Gabriel nodded enthusiastically. "That's exactly it!"

Schach slithered out of bed. "This must be a dream or a nightmare or maybe the tabouli we had for dinner. I'm going to the bathroom and see if all this passes." As he shuffled past Gabriel, he said, "If you want to give us a real miracle, put something good on TV every night. Bet ya can't do it." The bathroom door slammed shut. Schach groaned loudly, then moaned through the paper-thin walls, "Oh man, I'm never eating anything from a street vendor again!"

"Don't listen to him," Pandora said, leaning forward. "He's a sour grape. What this world really needs is a permanent half-off sale at

Nordstrom's. Now that would make a lot of people give thanks!"

"Oh, jeez," Schach whimpered as the other end of his anatomy cut loose a sound like an exploding whoopee cushion.

Pandora ignored the outburst. "And hairdressers who do what you tell them to do, not the latest thing they think is so great but would never do to their *own* hair." Pandora rested her hand on Gabriel's forearm. "Now if you could give us a skin cream that actually does remove wrinkles—Gabriel, just between you and me, that would be a real miracle!"

"I better write these down," Gabriel said as he fished a tablet and stylus from his pockets. "They're not quite what I expected; we must be even more out of touch than we realized. You're sure these things will prove divine existence to the subscribe—uh, people?"

"Absolutely. Oh, here's another, hair color that gets deep down into your roots so they don't show gray so fast."

"Flush, damn you!" Schach screamed. A moment later, he emerged from the bathroom and said, "Pandy, tomorrow morning we may need to use the bathroom in the lobby—" He stopped and stared at Gabriel. "You're still here?" Schach cautiously rubbed his stomach. "Maybe you're not the ghost of tabouli past. I thought once I woke up enough and, uh, unloaded, you'd be gone."

"I'm still here," Gabriel replied mildly.

"We're going to do some honest-to-God miracles," Pandora added, clapping her hands and giggling, "and everybody will be so happy."

"Yeah, everybody named Pandy," Schach muttered. "I heard what you told Gabriel. Why would a guy care about skin cream or department store sales?"

Gabriel furrowed his brow. "You mean these miracles won't prove divine existence to everyone?"

"Hell—heck no, nine-tenths of the world won't even *notice*," said Schach. "If you want people to pay attention, you've got to do something that hits all of them where they live."

"Um…in their homes?" Gabriel ventured.

Schach rolled his eyes. "That's not what I meant. The miracle has to be a big deal to them. It has to have meaning in their lives."

"Like turning a fish into enough fish to feed the multitudes?"

"Sort of, but if you did that today, the multitudes would probably sue you for mercury poisoning."

Gabriel's face sank into his hands, pushing up his cherubic cheeks. "What miracle could prove divine existence to everyone and get them praying again?" He looked up at Schach and Pandora. "It's impossible, isn't it?"

"What's wrong with a permanent half-off sale at Nordstrom's?" Pandora said. "Everybody would love it."

"Come on, Pandy, it has to be something everybody thinks is a miracle, not just you and your kaffee-klatsch."

"Nothing would satisfy you, you wet blanket. The only way you'd be happy is if you got your very own miracle!"

"My very own miracle?"

"Sure," Pandora replied. "While we're at it, why don't we give everyone their own personal miracle and a coupon for a free facial! You are such a brat, Schach."

"Pandy," Schach said, "I think you're on to something! What proves divine existence better than giving each person an individual miracle?"

"One miracle for each person on Earth?" said Gabriel dubiously.

"Why not? Everyone gets something they're sure is a miracle and confirms the divine existence of God. You get what you want and everyone else gets what they want. What could be better?"

"It's the democratic way," Pandora added. "One person, one miracle." She frowned. "But you should still do the permanent half-off sale at Nordstrom's miracle. You know," she leaned in and patted his knee, "as a show of good faith."

Gabriel shook his head. "It would never work. We couldn't service eight billion miracles at once. Engineering and technical support would kill us!"

"People wouldn't use them all at the same time," Schach replied. "A lot of people would save them for a rainy day." He frowned. "Hey…what do you mean engineering and technical support?"

"Never mind that. Think of the accounting nightmare," Gabriel whispered, his eyes de-focusing as he contemplated the paperwork.

"If convincing people God still exists is what you're after," Schach persisted, "won't this do it?"

"The thing is, what we really need—" Gabriel began, then caught himself and finished silently, *is prayer. Lots of it.*

"What do you really need?"

Gabriel considered whether it was kosher for the divine to beg or bargain with the great unwashed for prayer. The business model was predicated on the biogenerators' ignorance of their devotion's value as much as it was on their gullibility. If they found out they had been supplying power for entire worlds for thousands of years without so much as a thank you for payment, they might feel a tiny bit cheated. Gabriel carefully probed his sore back, remembering the reaction the last time these subscribers felt cheated.

"Gabriel?" Schach prodded.

"Would people pray for their miracles?" Gabriel asked. "Maybe, say, a month of nightly prayer and then you get your miracle?"

Schach shrugged. "Sure, why not? It would be worth it for a bona-fide miracle."

"If you made the exact waiting period a little fuzzy," Pandora added, "it would help you space out the miracles and you could do them all."

"There's no reason people need to choose a miracle up front," said Schach. "Let them pray for a month and when they've prayed enough, make it so they know they've earned their miracle. Then they can choose the miracle and have it performed at their leisure."

Pandora grinned. "It would be like a spiritual coupon with a one-per-person limit."

Gabriel shook his head. Things certainly had changed on Earth.

⏳ ⏳ ⏳ ⏳ ⏳

"If they pray every night for a month, they'll get into the habit of praying!" Gabriel argued. "Do you think they'll stop praying the night after their miracle occurs? Of course not! They'll be thankful."

"Hmmm." Jehovah stroked his beard as he paced the floor. "I don't know, Gabe. It's a ton of extra work, and as you yourself pointed out, it's an accounting nightmare." Jehovah shook his head slowly. "I don't think the Super will buy it. And I'm not sure I'm entirely keen on the idea myself."

"Well, let's at least ask the Super. It's not as if you have any ideas."

Jehovah stiffened for a moment. Unfortunately, Gabriel was right; he didn't have any ideas. "All right," he said sourly. "I'll call a meeting as soon as there's room on the Super's schedule."

"Fine," Gabriel said. "Whatever it takes to get this off my plate."

⌛   ⌛   ⌛   ⌛   ⌛

Gabriel kept trying to connect to start the meeting, but there seemed to be something wrong. The little angel icon on the screen just kept spinning with its annoyingly bright halo. Gabriel glanced nervously around the small, rectangular conference room. Michael looked bored. That butt-kisser Lucifer's lip curled down as he drummed his fingers on the table. Gabriel tried to ignore the cascading sound of Lucifer's infernal fingers, but he couldn't. What was Lucifer doing here anyway? This was none of his business.

Jehovah cleared his throat, straightened up in his chair, and said, "You know, Gabe, the Super's probably waiting for you to start the meeting and wondering what's going on."

"I know," Gabriel replied, trying and failing to keep the annoyance he felt over Lucifer and the madly spinning angel icon out of his voice. "I don't know if I can get this thing to work."

"Oh, come on, where's your faith, Gabe?" Jehovah said with a slight grin.

"Very funny," Gabriel muttered. "The presentation is teed up and ready to go, if only it would just connect." He pursed his lips, then brightened and said, "Ah, here we go!" as the angel stopped spinning and started dancing instead. The big screen in the conference room lit up and resolved into the image of the District Supervisor, with a thumbnail of the conference room and its occupants at the top of the screen above the District Supervisor's image.

Jehovah cleared his throat. "My apologies, District Supervisor, we were experiencing technical difficulties."

"Ether net problems again?" the District Supervisor asked.

"Haven't the slightest idea, I'm not much for technological details," Jehovah replied. "Anyway, Gabe here has an idea for how to handle the situation on Earth. It might work, but it would definitely take a lot of work to work. If you get my meaning."

"A lot of work, eh," said the District Supervisor, his eyes narrowing. "That usually means a lot of cost."

"It is a lot of work," Gabriel said. "But it's more of an investment than a cost, and it'll be worth it. Let me share my screen so you can see this too, District Supervisor." On the big screen in the conference room, the first slide replaced the District Supervisor, whose thumbnail joined the conference room thumbnail at the top of the screen. The slide depicted the decline of Earth's prayer power reservoir from a robust 200% in the good old days to about 20% now.

"Yes, yes, we know the situation is dire and the trend is very bad and so forth," the District Supervisor said. "Just tell me your idea and I'll tell you why we can't do it."

"Let me show you one more slide first." Gabriel clicked forward. The new slide was a motion slide that looped Pandora in the Jerusalem crowd, shouting, "Let's see some magic already! Let's see some magic already! Let's see some magic already!" After a few more loops, Gabriel paused it.

"They've strayed so far from our marketing brochure that they think miracles are garden-variety magic," Gabriel said. "They're desperate for miracles, for proof of divine existence." Gabriel spread his hands, his white robe draped from his arms like a sail. "It's simple," he said. "We give every subscriber who prays every day for a month their own personal miracle. Proof positive of the existence of God Almighty and the power of God Almighty. Once they're convinced of the existence of God and see the power of prayer in action, don't you think they'll keep praying?"

The District Supervisor leaned back in his chair. "An individual miracle for each and every one of the subscribers?"

"Right," said Gabriel. "If they pray every day for a month." Gabriel jumped up as the thought occurred to him. "And bonus, if they miss a day, they have to start over!"

"How many of them are there?"

"How many would you say?" Jehovah asked Gabriel.

"If every one of them does it," Lucifer cut in, "it's about eight billion."

"But they're not all subscribers!" Gabriel protested. "We have less than a third of them right now, and many of those in name only. It probably won't be more than two billion, tops." He shrugged. "Maybe three."

"Two or three billion individual miracles?" the District Supervisor said, his voice rising with each word.

"Two or three…billion…individual miracles?" Jehovah said, his voice cracking. "We…we could never support that!"

"But we could with the wild profits we'd make from the guaranteed month of prayer from every subscriber on Earth that takes up our offer! Plus, all the subscribers who generate enough prayer power to redeem for a miracle, but who choose to wait to use the miracle, will keep right on praying. How could they risk their miracle by stopping?" He took a deep breath. "And think of all the new subscribers we'll get as a result of this offer. There's never been anything like it!"

"That would give us some bang for the buck," Jehovah admitted. "But it's a lot of buck. And we couldn't let subscribers run around saving the world everywhere you look. We'd have to limit it to minor miracles, truly personal miracles. None of this world peace nonsense or curing world hunger or anything like that."

"Why not?"

Jehovah crossed his arms and frowned at Gabriel. "If we gave them all that stuff, what would they have left to pray for, eh?" He shook his head. "Honestly, Gabe."

"Okay, okay, you're right. But we have to give them miracles that they will recognize as being, well," Gabriel threw up his arms, "miraculous. A miracle isn't a miracle if it's just pouring water into a glass. It only becomes a miracle when you change the water into wine. We need to let them change some water into wine or their faith won't be rekindled and they won't start praying again."

"I hate to be the bad guy," Lucifer said, false regret tinging his tone. "I just attended the last Biogeneration Industry Conference Keynote Expert's Roundtable, less than an eternity ago." Gabriel rolled his eyes and thought, here we go, little show-off trying to get a promotion from angel to archangel by being a know-it-all and kissing frock. So he's been to BICKER, who cares?

Lucifer ignored Gabriel. "There was a very interesting Expert Panel discussion on the investment required in various biogeneration scenarios. It was a great panel, with Buddha, Vishnu, Allah, Odin, and Christ exchanging ideas and debating the effectiveness of various strategies." Lucifer took a sip of water while Gabriel silently cursed the little name-dropping toady.

"They came to the conclusion that you ought be able to find a way to put a little fear into them, whether it be physical fear, spiritual fear, or just a general unease about not praying. Maybe we should make an example out some of those who *don't* pray, a return to a little good old fashioned fire and brimstone."

Michael tittered. "Then there'll hardly be any of them left to pray!"

Lucifer ignored Michael and continued, "I know some freelance demons who could really change some attitudes. The Four Horsemen are on vacation, but when they get back, I'm sure they'd be happy to lend a hand."

Jehovah frowned. "It's become apparent that they've changed quite a bit since we used those marketing tactics, Lucifer."

Gabriel declared, "I say give them miracles and make them love you! It's the only thing they'll accept as evidence of divine existence. And unless they accept divine existence, they won't pray and we won't get their prayer power."

"Hmmm. I suppose," the District Supervisor said, "that we could let individuals have money, power, that sort of thing. Just as long as no planet-wide improvements relieve their everyday misery, that's all."

Jehovah sighed. "But we would have to evaluate each miracle. It's bound to be time-consuming. And we haven't got the staff for it."

"True," said Gabriel. "We might need some temporary staff. But if you have a better idea to bring the prayer power reservoir back to its normal level, be my guest."

An uncomfortable silence fell over the room.

"You know these subscribers, don't you, Jehovah? There must be something simpler we can do," said the District Supervisor.

"Hmmmph." Jehovah shook his head helplessly and tugged on his beard. "No, I can't think of a thing. Gabe and Mike were the ones who went there and saw what they're like now."

Michael shrugged. Any solution that meant he didn't have to go back down there was a good solution as far as he was concerned.

Gabriel arched an eyebrow. "I guess the only other idea is to watch the prayer power reservoir drop to zero."

The District Supervisor frowned. A reminder popped up in the corner of his screen about the friendly golf game with the District Supervisors of several other companies. In fact, one of the District Supervisors from the Hinduism Conglomerate owed him lunch from the last game. His thick, white eyebrows beetled. It wouldn't be fair to anyone to be late and muck up the game. Not a bit fair. He reached a decision.

"It's messy, but it gets around the problems of extensive market research and misfiring miracles. But let's make that prayer period a year, shall we, not just one month. No need to make it too easy on them or not to milk them for as much as we can."

"Great idea, District Supervisor!" Jehovah said.

"Ye-es," the District Supervisor agreed dryly. "Now if there's no further business?"

Lucifer opened his mouth but caught Jehovah's stern glare full in the face and snapped his jaw shut.

Several days later, the Archangel Gabriel appeared simultaneously to every person in the world and told them how to cash in on their very own personal miracle. Start praying *today*!

⌛ ⌛ ⌛ ⌛ ⌛ ⌛

"Mike! Hey, Michael!" Gabriel yelled. "Get a move on! The party's rockin' at Jehovah's place!" Gabriel shook his head. It was no wonder why Michael was the Archangel of Eternity; when it came to parties, he took one to get ready.

With the incoming flood of prayer energy had come praise from corporate headquarters and a noticeable lightening of the mood around the office. Gabriel couldn't remember seeing Jehovah so jovial, or *jeh-ovial*, as he liked to waggishly put it to his coworkers.

By the time Gabriel and Michael arrived at the party, Jehovah, Lucifer, and a bunch of minor functionary angels were on the banquet table doing a chorus line kick dance, their beards bouncing in time to their kicks. The angel at one end of the chorus line wore a lampshade, which he doffed every other kick to the revelers milling about the room and shouting encouragement to the dancers. Gabriel and Michael worked their way through the crowd to the giant punch bowl filled with sacramental wine, where Gabriel proceeded to ease the pain of the past days by really tying one on.

⧗   ⧗   ⧗   ⧗   ⧗

Once the first miracles had been confirmed, the party started on Earth, too. People who had never thought about religion were asking the devout about proper praying form; should the knees be together or apart? Hands at chest level or eye level? Nobody wanted to waste a year praying improperly and have to start over.

People prayed and prayed, until they had prayed enough to earn their miracles. Jehovah's prayer power reservoir rose like the water over the Titanic. People walked like gunslingers, with a loaded miracle in their pockets ready to fire off at any time. Every now and then one of the gunslingers whipped out a miracle and made a dream come true. Or a nightmare.

Jed Wistrow was in love. But alas, the object of his affection spurned his every effort with increasing scorn. So Jed used his miracle to make her marry him. She appeared at his side with a pop of displaced air, complete with a huge diamond ring on her finger, a flowing white wedding dress, and a bouquet. She looked up, down, and all around. She looked at Jed, then at the ring and the dress, and declared, "Afraid not, mister! I'm getting the hell out of here!" She threw the bouquet to the ground, closed her eyes and prayed to use her miracle, and with a pop of displaced air, she was gone, and so were two miracles. As the assembled guests stared at Jed standing alone at the altar feeling more naked than if he'd actually been naked, Jed swore off praying forever.

Daejong Woo could no longer stand the slow ascent up the corporate ladder. He knew exactly what was wrong with the company and exactly how to fix it. And now he had a way to do it. He closed his eyes and prayed to invoke his miracle. In an instant, he became the company President, CEO, and Chairman of the Board. Several disastrous decisions later, a company board member couldn't take it anymore, closed his eyes and fired off his miracle, and another two miracles were gone.

William Johnson bent at the waist, hands on knees, breathing like a Hoover on overdrive. Last again. He ran so hard, so hard, but here he was, last again. Again. Thank God he thanked God every night for a year, with a couple of months thrown in for good measure. He prayed mightily for superhuman speed, speed that would make The Flash seem like a slug.

William Johnson felt his body straighten up and his breath return, slow and even. He flexed his shoulders. He felt great! The quarter-mile track looked like he could take it in a stride. William Johnson grinned widely. He didn't even bother to take a stance, he just took off, intending to whip around the track and show them that even though he lost, if they dared to race him again, he'd win.

He felt more than saw his legs move. A disorienting blur masked his eyes. He stopped. He was on a city street. Bourbon Street. New Orleans. But that was impossible. He'd been in Flagstaff, Arizona less than a second ago. Was he really that fast? Better get back to Flagstaff. He took off again, but misjudged the distance and overshot Flagstaff by more than a state and a half and was now more than a little bit deep in the Pacific Ocean.

And so it went. People took things that didn't belong to them—or tried to—and then were forced to give them back.

⌛   ⌛   ⌛   ⌛   ⌛

"Wake up. Come on, wake up. I need to talk to you."

"Hey Schach," Pandora whispered sleepily, "I think it's that street swami again."

"The Archangel Gabriel," Gabriel reminded her helpfully.

"Don't you ever show up in the daytime?" Schach grumbled.

"I'm here because—heyyyy, wait a minute, you're both in the same bed again and you're still not married. One of you should be sleeping on the couch."

"That's okay, you can have it," said Schach through a yawn. "There're blankets in the hall closet. You can use a cushion for a pillow. G'night."

"Right, thanks." Gabriel started to get off the bed, then stopped, one leg hovering in mid-air over the floor. "Wait a minute. I have a question to ask you."

"Extra toilet paper's also in the hall closet," Schach murmured.

"Not that. I need to know why you stopped praying."

"Because it's three in the morning," Pandora whined. "We're trying to sleep."

"But you're not praying in the daytime, either."

Pandora said, "We already did our praying and we got our wishes."

"They're not wishes, they're *miracles*," Gabriel said, his voice rising.

"Wishes, miracles, whatever," said Pandora. "I wish I could go back to sleep now."

"Don't you people get it?" Gabriel crawled up the bed between Schach and Pandora until his face was a foot from theirs. "Divine existence has been proven unequivocally! You should be praying thankfully every day!"

"For what?" Schach asked. "The way most of these wishes turned out, nobody's sure just whose existence has been proven, anyway. If it's God, He's got a pretty sick sense of humor."

"But aren't you afraid of divine vengeance?" Gabriel spluttered.

"For what?" Schach scratched himself below the belt. "I didn't pray before and nothing happened. Why should it now?"

⌛   ⌛   ⌛   ⌛   ⌛

Jehovah tapped the power display panel with his forefinger, as if that might change the readings. He shook his head and thought, *oh bugger, the Super really isn't going to like this.*

S.L. LEITNER

I Am

The four of us are on our fifth scotch when Dave tugs his bushy brown beard and says, "You'll never guess what I invented."

Pete glares at his empty glass and ventures, "The bottomless scotch bottle?"

"No," Dave replies, "but almost as useful. My newest invention will revolutionize the world! It will change *everything*." Dave's right arm sweeps majestically out to us. "It will—"

"You'd better tell us what it is," I cut in, "or we're going to the bar to get another drink."

"Now wait a minute, guys!" Dave holds his palms out to keep us seated. "I'm not just talking about any old invention. I built a time machine!"

We stare for a moment, not even drinking. At last Bernie says incredulously, "A time machine?"

Dave nods and emphatically repeats, "A time machine."

"You're nuts!" Pete exclaims, then pushes back his lacquered oak chair and strides to the bar. With a tilt of my glass I drop the rest of the scotch down my throat, then join Pete for another refill, leaving Bernie to play with Dave—or Dave to play with Bernie. Bernie will listen to anything.

I pull up next to Pete and rest my elbows on the stained maroon pad that lines the front of the long oak bar. Raul, the bartender, notices me and grabs another glass.

"What do you think of this one?" I ask Pete.

Pete laughs and rolls his eyes, then accepts his scotch from Raul. "I think, well, um . . . that Dave's brain cells are about as loose as the ice in my whisky." He swirls the clinking cubes in the glass, then adds, "And they're melting at about the same rate."

When we return to our dark corner table, Bernie is saying, "You're really serious about this time machine, aren't you?"

"Of course I'm serious," Dave replies as we sit down. "When am I not serious? It was simply a matter of getting the—"

"Bull!" Pete interrupts. "I remember the time you invented a bona fide lead-to-gold converter. Brilliant, you said. A sure thing."

"The only sure thing," I add, "was that lump of twisted lead you wound up with."

"But this is different," Dave protests. "Just listen to me for a bit."

"Well, okay," Pete agrees, "but only because I'm too tipsy to know better."

"Give it a chance, you'll find that this makes perfectly good sense."

"Dave," says Pete, "everything you invent makes sense to you. You even make sense of what you say most of the time." Pete gulps the last half of his drink. "But what can you say to make sense of time travel?" Pete nods knowingly at his empty glass.

"What about the 'ol kill-your-own-grandfather paradox?" I ask. "If I go back in time and—"

"Don't think about time like that!" Dave breaks in.

"Then how *should* we think about time?" Bernie asks.

I roll my eyes in a *here we go* look and Dave dives in like a barracuda. "Think about this: time is the fourth dimension. Shapes, forms—*life* in the other three dimensions can be rearranged or altered, either chemically or physically. I believe shapes and forms in the dimension of time can be changed too, so—"

"What does changing shape have to do with time travel?" Bernie interrupts. Bernie is a nice guy, but he can be drawn into any dumb discussion with Dave. Before Dave can hook us, Pete and I escape and head back to the bar.

ORIGINATION

⌛   ⌛   ⌛   ⌛   ⌛

An unknown number of drinks later, Dave talks us into going to his place to see the time machine. Fortunately, Dave's wife Doris is a sound sleeper; even so, the lamp we run into in the living room makes a really loud noise when we accidentally introduce it to an end table.

"I'll clean up that broken glass later," Dave whispers and hustles toward the door to the basement. We scamper after him.

Bernie trots down the steep staircase like a mountain goat, right after Dave. I might have had one or five more scotches than Dave and Bernie, so I take it a bit easier. "Wow, you've cleared out half the lab," I hear Bernie say as I clutch the rail and fish around with my toe for the next narrow step. "I need the open space for a transit area," Dave replies.

I reach the bottom and exhale. That wasn't too bad, now that I'm on the basement's nice, not-narrow, level concrete. On the otherwise empty right side of the basement, fluorescent orange tape on the floor marks off a rectangle big enough to hold a Cadillac. All Dave's usual tools, machines, scopes, and other playthings are crammed into the left half of the basement.

"So where's the fabled time machine?" I ask.

"Right here," Dave replies, opening a drawer and pulling out a slim black box that looks like a Star Trek tricorder with a few added knobs.

"That's your time machine?" I ask with a shake of my head.

"I hope you don't have to get in it to use it," Pete cracks.

Dave winces a pained *why me* look, then points to the taped-off area. "All you have to do is stand in that box. Don't worry, guys," he hastily reassures, "it's safe. I'm gonna try it out on some lab rats tomorrow."

"Tomorrow?" Bernie asks. "You want to try it out on us now and on some rats tomorrow?"

"Oh, come on," says Pete, "you can't take him seriously! This is all a load of bull."

"Yeah, you don't think this could actually work, do you?" I ask. "You're *four* sheets to the wind if you believe this crap."

"Then why don't you two just step into the box, since nothing's going to happen," Bernie replies.

"One at a time, one at a time!" Dave admonishes, holding up a hand. "You'll all get your chance."

"Um," I mutter intelligently.

"Why don't you two flip a coin?" Bernie suggests.

"Why don't *we three* draw lots?" I suggest.

"Because I'm not drunk enough or dumb enough to try this."

"But you and me," Pete says, swaying against me in a perfect drunken sailor parody, "we got the perfect qualif . . . qualificakesh . . . we . . ."

"Right, Pete. Lucky us," I agree sourly as sobriety begins to tug at my consciousness.

"Here," Bernie says, "I've got a coin. Call it in the air. Winner's choice."

"Sounds like a race horse," Pete says.

"I hope not. I never pick the right pony."

"Call it in the air," Bernie insists, flipping the coin.

I call heads.

Bernie uncovers the coin and declares, "Tails."

"You're up, lucky man!" Pete says, then starts giggling.

"Don't we have to prepare anything?" I ask Dave. "Or wait until the moon is in the right position or something?"

"No," Dave replies, "we're set to go now. Just step right into the taped-off box." He shoos at me with his right hand while studying the time machine controls.

"Give my regards to H.G. Wells," Pete says, and laughs. The effects of the alcohol fade as I wonder why the hell I am standing in the box. Of course, time travel is impossible, so I have nothing to fear. And everything Dave invents screws up in some way or another. This can't possibly work. I'm sure nothing will happen. Well, maybe Dave's control box will short-circuit with some fizzing and sparks and then melt into a glob. But nothing will happen to *me*.

Dave starts to fiddle with the controls on the little black box. The guys move as if they're slogging through molasses. Pete is slowly doubling over with laughter at one of his own sarcastic comments. I can distinguish each separate sound of Pete's laughter as he makes it; I perceive each small movement separately. The last things I see are looks of astonishment from Pete, Bernie . . . and Dave.

ORIGINATION

I slowly tear apart. Each individual, physical, mental, and spiritual element of my essence explodes in slow motion, but I am not dead! But where am I? I can't see, smell, hear, touch—nothing. Then . . . "What happened to ME?" I scream with no voice.

All I can do is think and remember—remember Dave talking about chemically or physically changing shape and form in time.

Suddenly, I become whole, yet not whole. In an instant, an essence of myself, my spirit—my soul—emerges within every living person in the world. But not only in the "present" time, in every time. I am Caesar . . . and I am Brutus. I am Dave and Pete and Bernie and Raul. I am everyone you knew, everyone you know, and everyone you will know, everywhere and everywhen.

So get up and pour yourself a drink, because I'm thirsty.

S.L. LEITNER

The Gardener

"Oh, the egaliplasty!" Aristocrat Bleen cried.

"The what?" said Aristocrat Actiban. "What is egaliplasty?"

"It's just egaliplasty and it means boredom! I made it up because I'm bored!"

"It's true," agreed Aristocrat Cadifagle. "You're bored. I'm bored. We're all bored. Everything is the same, same, same, all the time, every time."

"You've said that before," said Aristocrat Actiban.

"Case in point, then."

"But what can we do about it?" cried Aristocrat Bleen, stretching out on the chaise longue in a manner that Aristocrat Bleen deemed dramatic. "Reality is constant."

"No it's not," said Aristocrat Actiban.

"It's constantly boring," said Aristocrat Bleen, pleased that Actiban had fallen for the little trap. "Everything *is* the same, same, same, all the time, every time. We made this reality ages ago and it's wearing on me. It's time we moved on and made a new reality."

"But that's such a long process," said Aristocrat Cadifagle. "It'll take forever to reseed The Garden, and then what do we do with this reality? It's hardly mature."

"We use it as raw material for the new reality, of course," said Aristocrat Bleen. "That'll make reseeding The Garden much faster. Waste not, want not."

"Hmmm; I wonder how reusing the material will affect the new reality—and isn't that a lot of material to start with?" asked Aristocrat Actiban. "Aristocrat Cadifagle, if we put all the mass of this reality into one seed to make a new reality, what would happen?"

"Into one seed?"

Actiban nodded.

"All of the mass? Including ourselves?"

Actiban paused. That had not been considered. But why not? It might be interesting to see what happened. Certainly not boring. Actiban nodded slowly. "Yes, including ourselves."

Cadifagle froze for several moments, like a glitch in a streaming movie. Then Cadifagle continued as if there had been no pause. "If we squeeze all that mass down into one seed, when we trigger the new reality, it'll burst out of that seed faster than anything we've ever experienced."

"Oh, good!" exclaimed Aristocrat Bleen. "A new experience! What will it be like?"

Cadifagle's form rippled. "We haven't experienced it yet, so I don't know."

"But you're sure it'll work? I'll blame you if it's not entertaining."

Cadifagle's form rippled again. "It won't be like the way we created this reality or previous realities, piece by piece until we ran out of energy. It'll be fast—really, really fast—and it'll release a lot of energy so we'll be able to make a lot of matter. But I think we might not have much control over it; it'll happen that fast."

"Marvelous!" said Bleen.

"I'm beginning to be unsure about this," said Actiban. "I don't like the idea of not having complete control of the process."

Bleen radiated the warm energy of excitement. "It'll be fine. You worry too much. Cadifagle, will we see this creation as it happens? Or will it happen so quickly that we'll just find ourselves inside it?"

"I don't know." Cadifagle's tone held a slightly impatient edge. "We haven't experienced it yet."

"Well, if we don't like it," Bleen replied, "we can always start again and do it the slow, old fashioned way. Let's tell The Gardener to get started on that seed." Aristocrat Bleen's thoughts reached out, not directly for The Gardener, but instead for The Butler. Proper process was required in all things, especially when those things were the commands of The Aristocrats.

The Aristocrats watched as Bleen instantiated The Butler. Matter that wasn't being used for anything important in their currently established reality converted to energy that coalesced before them in a brilliant swirl of sparkling colored light. Then the energy converted back to matter and manifested in the form of the construct known as The Butler. The Butler oscillated in an obsequious manner and said in a flat tone without inflection, "What is your command?"

Aristocrat Bleen explained what they wanted The Gardener to do. Aristocrat Cadifagle added, "We will instantiate you periodically to check on and report The Gardener's progress." The Butler oscillated again and then went to communicate with The Gardener.

⧖   ⧖   ⧖   ⧖   ⧖

The Gardener looked around The Garden in some annoyance after The Butler delivered the edict. "But it's been this way forever!" The Gardener complained. "Forever!"

As far as The Gardener knew, this was true. Because The Gardener was not an Aristocrat, there was no awareness of previous realities, only the reality for which The Gardener had been instantiated to attend. The Gardener had been The Gardener since the beginning of existence, as far as The Gardener knew or was concerned. And The Garden had been the same the whole time. And The Gardener had tended it the same way. The Gardener had just uprooted a bright orange and red bulb on one edge of The Garden to fix a budding supernova on one edge of the universe. The bulb dropped unnoticed to The Garden's rough bed as The Gardener wrestled with The Aristocrats' command.

The Garden was healthy. It reflected the energy of every corner of the universe. If anything went wrong anywhere, The Garden showed where the problem was and The Gardener could tend to it until The Garden, and thus the universe, was healed. The Gardener neither knew nor questioned how or why the faithful tending of The Garden resulted in the faithful tending of the universe. This was how it was, how it had always been, and how it would always be. And how it should be.

Until now.

The Gardener didn't understand that The Aristocrats used The Garden to grow new energy until there was enough to sculpt a new reality, complete with a new Garden and a new Gardener crafted specifically for that particular reality. When The Aristocrats tired of a reality, they had always taken the time to grow as many new seeds as they needed from which to build a new reality. Then they had abandoned the old reality to devolve and die a natural, entropic death. The idea of using the old reality to create a new one hadn't occurred to them because novel ideas didn't come easily to beings as entrenched in their supreme ways as The Aristocrats and because a fully mature reality contained a lot of energy that would be difficult to control.

The Butler's form rippled. "It is the command of The Aristocrats. We exist to serve them."

"I know," said The Gardener, looking at The Garden with some sadness. "I'll get started on it. It'll take a while; there's a lot of matter to gather." The Gardener looked back at The Butler. "One seed, they said?"

"One seed," The Butler confirmed.

"Seems unnecessarily tricky," The Gardener said. "Potentially unstable."

The Butler's form rippled again. "The Aristocrats command it."

"So they do, so they do." The Gardener noticed the dropped red and orange bulb and scooped it up before it could take root again and cause trouble in the universe.

The Gardener worked with reluctant diligence. The first thing was to find a suitable seed. Because The Aristocrats willed it, The Gardener had faith that eventually a seed capable of holding the energy of the entire universe would appear, and eventually it did. The Gardener gathered the

ORIGINATION

matter of the universe, one corner at a time, converted it back to energy, and then stored it in the seed. The seed didn't grow in size, but The Gardener could feel it growing in every other way, becoming denser and denser and hotter and hotter, yet remaining dormant within its opaque brown coat.

The Gardener needed no nourishment or rest, so The Gardener worked continuously at the same steady pace, gathering matter and storing it as energy, then gathering more matter and storing it as energy. Although The Aristocrats could have communicated with The Gardener in any way they could imagine, it pleased them to use The Butler. This was the sort of proper procedure that propped up both the universe and The Aristocrats' sense of self-importance, developed over countless eons in countless universes.

"How are you proceeding?" The Butler inquired.

The Gardener looked up from packing some energy into the seed. "Not long now. Probably there's only about a quarter of the matter left to convert, maybe a bit less. When I'm done, I'll come and get The Aristocrats and put them in the seed too."

"No." The Butler's form rippled a moment as The Aristocrats communicated their wishes. "You will inform me when you are ready and I shall escort The Aristocrats to The Garden."

"It's all the same to me." If The Gardener could have shrugged, The Gardener would have shrugged. The Gardener finished packing the latest batch of converted energy into the shell. "I'll tell you when I'm done." The Gardener went to gather more of the universe's remaining matter.

The Butler shimmered and then faded away.

⌛   ⌛   ⌛   ⌛   ⌛

As The Gardener packed more and more converted matter into the seed, the seed's coat strained more and more to contain the energy. Eventually, The Gardener had gathered every bit of mass in the universe, including everything around The Aristocrats, but not The Aristocrats themselves, and packed it into the seed.

The Gardener stared at his handiwork, the only thing left in The Garden, feeling an ownership that he had never felt before. His handiwork. His. Was he a he? Somehow, he was no longer just The Gardener, doing his job for The Aristocrats in their Garden as ever and always; he was something more. He was still The Gardener, but also he, or maybe she. The Gardener had confusing feelings of maternity and paternity about the seed as well, or maybe The Seed. The Seed, which contained all the matter in the universe except The Aristocrats and himself. He had mothered and fathered it, and as he stared, The Seed's coat began to glow with the growing heat within it.

The Gardener knew that he should call The Butler to fetch The Aristocrats, but he couldn't seem to will it. Instead, he watched in fixed fascination as the coat started to quiver and undulate with the barely contained energy. The Seed's brown coat could no longer hide the radiance of the heat caused by the incredible density of energy within. The coat began to glow with an orange-yellow hue. It transformed gradually to a darker blue, then a lighter blue, and then it blossomed into blinding white.

The Gardener felt more than saw energy trying to leak through The Seed's coat and tried frantically to stuff the energy back down, pack it back into The Seed, but the coat was wavering and giving way to the blinding white energy. The Gardener worked furiously to cram the errant energy back into The Seed's coat, but instead became entangled with The Seed, unable to break away. The Gardener called out for The Butler, but there had been a slight miscalculation. There was no longer matter in the universe from which to instantiate The Butler; it was all in The Seed.

Help? The Gardener thought.

"Help!" The Gardener screamed.

⧖   ⧖   ⧖   ⧖   ⧖

"Did somebody cry for help without going through The Butler first?" asked Aristocrat Actiban.

"I heard it too," said Aristocrat Bleen.

Then what was left of the universe—The Aristocrats—for an

infinitesimal moment seemed sucked toward The Garden. The moment ended, and if The Aristocrats had had ears, they would have covered them. Something whizzed by The Aristocrats at the boundary of their speed of event detection with a sonic boom to end all sonic booms.

"What was that?" cried Aristocrat Bleen.

"I don't know," replied Aristocrat Cadifagle. "What *was* that?"

"I'll call The Butler," said Aristocrat Actiban. After a moment, Actiban said, "Oh no, something's wrong. I can't call the Butler."

"And you know," said Aristocrat Bleen, "it does seem a bit, well, *empty* around here."

⧖   ⧖   ⧖   ⧖   ⧖

Just as The Seed's coat completely enveloped The Gardener, The Seed blew up far more spectacularly than The Gardener could ever have imagined. In fact, The Gardener was too busy hurtling headlong, screaming and flailing, one with the front of an eternally expanding omni-dimensional wave, to imagine anything beyond the sheer terror of the actual experience.

The new universe continued to expand. The energy instantiated into the matter known as The Gardener gradually grew tired of panicking and began to pay attention to something other than fear, riding the edge of the expansion in all directions and all dimensions simultaneously. In the same simultaneous way, The Gardener was everywhere the wave had passed, seeing everything that had happened and continued to happen, everywhere, at every moment of the endless expansion. Time lost its association with duration and experience, and effectively ceased to exist for The Gardener, who stretched like everlasting omni-directional elastic across the universe, covering it and experiencing its totality, yet neither restricting it nor being visible in it.

As the boundless energy slowed and cooled, it began to transform into matter and coalesce into objects. The objects varied greatly. Some were organic, some were inorganic. Objects seemed to float in space, cool and rocky or warm and gaseous or hot and fiery; some rotated around others, some streaked through the blackness almost as fast as The Gardener, and some smashed into each other in catastrophic cataclysms.

Some of the large objects seemed to house smaller objects, much, much smaller objects. The Gardener—or perhaps he or perhaps she or perhaps both—watched in fascination as an assortment of organic objects began to create other organic objects. The objects either divided themselves into multiple new organisms or briefly joined themselves, only to split apart again and somehow create one or more new organisms in addition to the original organisms. The new organisms seemed to grow, and in turn, replicate of their own accord instead of having to be made from some spare energy grown in The Garden. The Gardener understood instantiation but had never seen or conceived of anything like procreation.

⧖ ⧖ ⧖ ⧖ ⧖

"You're right," Aristocrat Cadifagle agreed. "It does seem a bit empty around here, in fact, more than a bit. We seem to be the only energy I can sense."

"The Garden is gone!" Aristocrat Bleen cried. "The Gardener is gone! All of our universe is gone!"

"You…you mean The Gardener stole our universe?" Aristocrat Actiban spluttered.

"It appears so," said Aristocrat Cadifagle. "That means The Gardener is God and we're…we're…I don't know what we are."

"But we were supposed to be God!" Aristocrat Bleen wailed. "We're always God! And it was our energy in the first place! It grew in our Garden and we're the ones who used it to create a new reality. It's rightfully ours and The Gardener stole it!"

"The nerve!" Aristocrat Actiban shouted. "We'll just have to create another universe!"

If Aristocrat Cadifagle could have blanched, Aristocrat Cadifagle would have blanched. "From what? There's no Garden. We're the only energy here."

"You said it would work!" Bleen wailed.

"I said we hadn't experienced it yet so we couldn't know what would happen," Cadifagle replied. "Nothing was guaranteed."

"Bleen, if you hadn't been so damned bored we never would have done this," Actiban said. "It's your fault and it's Cadifagle's fault for telling us we could do it. I never would have approved of it otherwise."

Cadifagle focused on Actiban. "Since when is your approval paramount?"

"I am the one—"

"Stop!" exclaimed Aristocrat Bleen. "What are we going to do?"

The three Aristocrats stared at each other. They edged slightly farther away from one another, like rival gunfighters trapped in a corral with no exit. Cadifagle sized up the other two Aristocrats and wondered just how much energy it did take to start up a little universe.

Behind the Scenes

Dear Sir or Madam, will you read my book?
It took me years to write, will you take a look?
    —*The Beatles, Paperback Writer*

Some people like to know just what in the wide world of sports the author was thinking when the author wrote a particular story. What sparked the idea? Where did that character come from? If fiction is truth shrouded in lies, what truth?

Some people are curious about elements of the story. What did "x" mean? Why an old puke-green Plymouth? Did the Swiss really set a speed trap for visiting Liechtensteiners? C'mon, food fights are urban myths—they only happen in movies.

Behind the Scenes reveals some of the inanity bouncing around in the cavernous hollow spaces between a writer's ears, crashing into the few logical thoughts that hang by metaphysical threads in the writer's consciousness and shredding them to bits.

These stories span most of my fiction-writing lifetime. Here's a rough chronology of when the initial version of each story was finished:

- High School: *I Am*
- College: *Secret Agent Emily, Davi, Creating a Masterpiece*
- 1990s: *Blanque's Suburbia, Every Mad Dog Has His Day*
- 2010s: *Showtime at the Apocalypse Theater, The Irate Businessman*
- 2020s: *Achoo!, The Great Cafeteria Food Fight and Ice Cream Raid of 1981, The Gardener, Scrimshaw Jones*

From college graduation until deep into the 1990s, I focused mainly on my new vocation (technical writing) and being a numbnut. During the 2000s and much of the 2010s, I wrote very little fiction because I was busy being a dad.

Oh, by the way, in the introduction, I lied. There *is* a test and this *will* be on it.

Behind the Scenes of Showtime at the Apocalypse Theater

Showtime at the Apocalypse Theater is based on a true event. Not the nuclear war—not yet, anyway—the speeding tickets.

As depicted in the story within the story, the Swiss really did lower the speed limit coming into Switzerland from Liechtenstein. And they really did remove the speed limit signs and ticket Liechtensteiners driving into Switzerland. Liechtenstein's real-life protest was a bit different than in the story, and nuclear catastrophe was, narrowly, averted. Even though the outer story of the Historian and World War III isn't true as of this writing, the world is working on it like the madmen we are.

This story is an example of one of my favorite ways of ideating a story: finding a relationship between two apparently unconnected ideas or events, in this case, finding a relationship between Switzerland setting speed traps for Liechtensteiners and World War III.

I wrote the first version of this story not long after reading about the speeding ticket fiasco.

As a point of curiosity, some of you might wonder how Switzerland got their hands on a nuclear bomb. When you have a lot of money, a lot of scientists, and nobody thinks you're up to something, it's not that hard. (Today, the Swiss are, in point of fact, the greatest nuclear power on the face of the Earth, but nobody knows it because, c'mon, the *Swiss? Really?* Such is the power of anonymity.)

The Swiss developed their nuclear capability under the cover of an operating cheese factory tucked into a rural valley among dairy farms. Scientists came and went disguised as cheese technology consultants, ostensibly tasked with making the holes in the cheese align in regular, orderly patterns. This seemed perfectly sensible for a people who swept the fronts of their stores and houses daily and insisted on having the most accurate clocks in the world.

Parts were delivered hidden in large wheels of cheese ostensibly sent to the factory for packaging into consumer-ready chunks, submerged in giant vats of milk, and even sequestered inside a few unlucky cows. The smell of cheese overwhelmed the smell of oils and lubricants used in the nuclear development center hidden under the cheese factory, so nobody was the wiser. If they had been caught, the plan was to say that they were making the world's largest nuclear cuckoo clock, and in a very Swiss style of Maltese Falcon manner, were going to conceal the nuclear cuckoo clock in a coating of Gruyère.

Although this is lost in the annals of history, it is true that Liechtenstein also had a nuclear bomb, which they developed under no cover whatsoever, because, hell, they're *Liechtenstein*; nobody was paying attention to them anyway.

Behind the Scenes of Achoo!

Achoo! is based on a true event. Although there is no Junior College of American Pathology, in the 2000s, the CDC sent a virus test kit to more than 5,000 partner labs. The kit accidentally contained a sample of a very nasty live virus from the 1910s that they believed could lead to a pandemic if unleashed on the uninoculated public. They really did contact the labs that received the deadly virus and ask them to pretty please destroy it. Fortunately, it turned out that due to fighting various flus over the decades, humankind had gained enough immunity to make the accidentally delivered virus a big nothing-burger.

When I read the articles about the accidental release, I couldn't help envisioning the response from labs all over the world when the CDC asked them to return the deadly virus. I wrote the scenes with the French, Lebanese, and Swiss labs then and there, but I didn't have a story to go around them. When COVID hit, it sparked me to revisit those scenes. When I did, the question arose, "Who is calling the labs? And how did the poor sucker get saddled with *that* job?" The story grew organically from that point and the Junior College of American Pathology was born in 2020.

If anyone takes offense at the portrayals of lab personnel, please remember that this story is one long joke at the expense of the Junior College of American Pathology, which, as previously mentioned, doesn't exist. In fact, the College of American Pathology doesn't exist. There is, however, a College of American Pathologists, a legitimate organization of board-certified pathologists. The College of American Pathologists was not a model for my College of American Pathology and I hope the good people doing good work there take no offense at my bit of fun. After all, it was the CDC that shipped the live virus, not the College of American Pathologists.

    I might have an extra bit of fun with the French, but don't we all? That the French revere Jerry Lewis shows they have a twisted and warped enough sense of humor to take the joke. Besides, when you have the best food and wine in the world, you shouldn't let little things bother you.

Behind the Scenes of Davi

Davi is one of three stories in this collection that I wrote in college. I didn't have a word processor then, and if I had, it wouldn't have had a font suitable for Davi's handwriting. I wrote Davi's original script by hand, using my non-writing hand, which was a challenge to match with the typed portions of the text.

For the first draft, I alternated each page between hand writing and typing as I wrote it, which wasn't so bad.

What was so bad was putting them together and the rewrites. If I wanted to rewrite or move just one line, it meant not only retyping pages of text, it meant handwriting pages of Davi's handwriting all over again. What was worse, the handwriting with my non-writing hand was getting better and looking less like Davi's script with every iteration, so I had to work harder at making it a scrawl with each change. I did a lot of retyping and rehandwriting. A *lot* of retyping and rehandwriting. Suffice to say, I'm grateful for the choice of fonts we have these days and the fact that I haven't touched a typewriter since college.

When I wrote *Davi*, I was fed up with some sort of bureaucratic nonsense that I no longer recall because college days were stuffed full of bureaucratic nonsense. (Sadly, madly, badly, it turned out that the real world is too. So much for hiding out in college for a few years. That ol' reality gonna hunt ya down and getcha.) The bureaucrats even took seven percent right off the top of my student loans for "insurance", thus helping insure that it was even harder to do inconsequential things such as pay rent, pay tuition, buy books, and occasionally even eat food. Well, boxes of off-brand mac & cheese on sale eight for a buck, if you're generous enough to call that food. We balked at even calling it sustenance and settled instead for the term gut filler.

My sense from college and everything after is that, whatever else happens, it won't be just the cockroaches that survive. The bureaucrats and the bureaucracy will remain too, the human equivalent of cockroaches, and we will remain subservient to them because if we don't, then they'll really screw up our lives.

Behind the Scenes of Secret Agent Emily

Secret Agent Emily is based on real events and is another story I wrote in college. The events took place in San Francisco around 1983 or so. I didn't know "Emily" (Emily wasn't the name of the victim and I invented Emily's friend Mabel), so I don't know what she really thought when she found out she'd been taken for her life savings. When I read the story in the newspaper (yes, newspaper), I was horrified that anyone would do that to someone. This was, of course, long before there were internet scams preying on the elderly to send money to get their grandson out of jail or help a prince free up a huge sum of cash if only you could send some cash first, so this was not a common story.

Then my sick mind started wondering if there was some way for "Emily" to make lemonade out of those bitter, bitter lemons, and *Secret Agent Emily* was born.

I wouldn't call *Secret Agent Emily* a story that's representative of my usual subject matter, if indeed I have usual subject matter, but it does represent that stories can come to a writer from anywhere, at any time (this idea came over morning coffee), and from any circumstances.

It seems unrealistic that Emily got double-dipped, and even though it seemed to me to stretch the bounds of fictional credibility, it happened in real life and continues to happen today. I see stories of even highly-educated people getting taken for everything they have when scammers talk them into going back to their financial accounts over and over again until they're drained. Some of them say that once they started, they just couldn't stop even if they started to question what was happening. They got sucked into the confidence game and felt just like Emily—alive for once in a world that had forgotten them. Life is often less credible than fiction, yet, self-evidently, often stranger.

Behind the Scenes of Creating a Masterpiece

Creating a Masterpiece is the last of three stories in this collection that I wrote in college. It won an award (and 100 delightful smackers) in the 1984 Early Universe Science Fiction Writing Contest, open to all University of California students. There were three cash prizes. I was the only undergrad to win one. Another winner was my classmate in Kim Stanley Robinson's creative writing class at UC Davis, Gary Konas. I have no idea what Gary or most of my classmates did later in terms of writing, except for Karen Joy Fowler. Karen writes fiction, has published many novels and short stories, and has won many awards, including the Nebula Award.

In addition to the class, Kim—Stan to most of his friends and family, Kim to all of us at UC Davis; I was never quite sure what to read into that—skimmed the cream off the top of his creative writing class and started a UC Davis writers group that met at someone's apartment, it might have even been Kim's; recollection gets a bit sepia-tinged after four decades. Kim's group was a great place to critique each other's stories and grow as writers.

Creating a Masterpiece came about when I needed a story to submit to Kim's class and I needed it fast. Nothing suggested itself. I took a figurative step back (my apartment was so small that if I had taken a literal step back,

I'd have been next door) and asked myself, "What are you doing?" The answer that echoed back in my mind was, "Creating a masterpiece. What else would I be doing, creating a mediocre piece?" Asking that question kicked off the story. The characters quickly made themselves known and took over. Sometimes I craft a story every step of the way. Other times, the characters shove me aside and take control while I watch and write down what happens. This is one of those where I mostly watched and wrote down what happened, because I didn't know until I saw it happen in my mind's eye.

The old Plymouth steel tank at the end of the story is an homage to my first car, a dented, puke-green 1966 Plymouth Fury II Belvedere with a 318 engine block bored down to 273. I bought the car from a neighbor for $50. It was barely hobbling along on four of its eight cylinders. I limped it in to my high school auto shop, every moment expecting it to give out in the middle of the street, or worse, at the entrance to the high school parking lot. I imagined the engine sputtering and coughing, then dying with a bang and a cloud of blue smoke, the car left blocking the parking lot entrance like a beached whale while honking vehicles piled up behind me and jeering spectators piled up in front of me. But my good old Plymouth made it. I spent every hour I could for the next two and half months rebuilding the engine under the watchful guidance of our wonderful automotive teacher, Henry Robles. I got most of the parts from scouring through junkyards full of rusty old boat-sized cars.

Mr. Robles insisted that every part be cleaner than your silverware before it went into the car. I spent a week and a half polishing piston heads and thinking I would never be able to sand out the shadow of oil stains past, but Mr. Robles wouldn't take, "It'll never come out, this is useless!" as an answer. Of course, he was right; eventually, the stains came out and those piston heads shone like brand new. By the time I was done rebuilding that engine, it was at least as good as new, maybe better, and as clean as could be. That was probably as close as I'll come to creating a masterpiece.

Behind the Scenes of Blanque's Suburbia

I wrote the first draft of *Blanque's Suburbia* more than a decade after I wrote *Creating a Masterpiece*, the story in which I introduced the narrator character. So far, this narrator is my only character to appear in multiple stories—he's in three stories in this book. *Blanque's Suburbia* is the first sequel to *Creating a Masterpiece*. (*Scrimshaw Jones* is the next story in what has become a series.)

I'm fascinated with what lies in the shadows. Not just the darkness in the light, but also the shadows we create in our minds; shadows of uncertainty, shadows of insecurity, shadows of paranoia. That's why I love the Twilight Zone so much, especially Rod Serling's original incarnation and Jordan Peele's reboot. Peele really channels Serling and understands what lies in the shadows.

I'm especially fascinated with the intersection of physical and psychological shadows. *Blanque's Suburbia* plays like an oblivious child in that busy intersection, never mind the chance of being flattened by a metaphysical bus.

The idea for *Blanque's Suburbia* came to me after I reread *Creating a Masterpiece*. I wondered what other artist friends the narrator knew. I leaned back on the couch, closed my eyes, and let the narrator enter my consciousness. Where was the narrator? It turned out that he was walking down a sleepy suburban street, on the way to visit another artist friend.

Perfect!

    I watched the narrator and felt his thoughts trickle into my mind. In his world, it had been only a few days since the events in *Creating a Masterpiece*, while in my world, it had been more than a decade. The first draft of the story came quickly as the narrator took over, with me-the-writer more as me-the-observer again, writing down what happened and what the narrator saw and thought. Nothing was planned or plotted. Sometimes stories spill out like that.

    I can't explain where Blanque came from or why she was a performance artist. Blanque was simply the friend the narrator was visiting, the person who answered the door when the narrator showed up. After I wrote *Blanque's Suburbia*, I toyed with the idea of the narrator being a sort of Flying Dutchman who haunts not doomed ships, but doomed artists. I liked the narrator character and wanted to write more of his stories. But I was concerned that the endings might be too obvious, so I didn't write more. It took three decades because I can be a bit slow, but I eventually realized that in just about every detective novel, the detective solves the murder. You know that as a reader, but it's not about knowing the murder will be solved in the end, it's about how you get there, the story and the characters and the bits of truth about life. This sort of thing is true of many genres. So the narrator eventually returned to the pads of my keyboard in the most recent of my stories, *Scrimshaw Jones*.

    One of the lines I worked on the most in *Blanque's Suburbia* was the last line of the story. Egotistically, I like to think that one of my eight favorite authors, Edgar Allan Poe, would have appreciated that last line. I hope it raises a goosebump or two.

Behind the Scenes of Scrimshaw Jones

Origination was supposed to have eleven stories, not twelve. One night late in 2024, after polishing up *Creating a Masterpiece* and *Blanque's Suburbia* for the book, I was up late watching one of my three favorite sports, Australian Rules Football. Sort of. Mainly, I was inside my own head, thinking about two things.

I was lamenting that the narrator of those two stories would never have a new story, that *Blanque's Suburbia* was his curtain call.

I was simultaneously ruminating about an idea for a book of short stories that I had come up with while flying to Texas in October, 2023. Looking down from 30,000 feet, I saw trails everywhere, bereft of travelers, leading from no place to nowhere, criss-crossing through dusty dirt, rock outcroppings and tors, ravines, and mesas, all shades of brown and dark red, dotted by dark green scrub brush. It reminded me of a cousin, the Australian Outback, and I understood that this was the American Outback.

I wondered who or what traversed that random looking mish-mash of trails with no apparent beginning or end. The American Outback encompasses large swathes of places like west Texas, New Mexico, Arizona, Utah, and Nevada, and even beyond. There must be as many stories as there are trails…

As these two subjects intertwined in my mind, I heard the game announcer say the name of a player named Scrimshaw. I don't know why, but that combination, triggered by the name Scrimshaw, spawned this story. Unlike the first two in the series, the whole of the story came to me over the next bit of time and I knew where it went from the start. I finished the story in 2025, just in time to include in this book.

I think this, my most recent story, represents my best writing craftsmanship to date. I don't know if I'll write more stories about the American Outback or if I'll write enough of them for a book, but at least now there's one.

Behind the Scenes of Every Mad Dog Has His Day

I wrote *Every Mad Dog Has His Day* in the late 1990s. This story is fictional, but it should be noted that it took three people to get that dummy over the fence, not two. Of course, taking a dummy from a fireman's training center is illegal and I would never encourage or engage in that sort of behavior and this is fiction. Obviously. Never mind that I mentioned in the introductory blather that fiction is truth shrouded in lies.

Had a dummy been liberated, I suspect it would have been involved in or indeed masterminded several adventures in and around a certain fictional dormitory that might have been hallucinated, or at least hallucinated in, by some of its residents. I say masterminded because few of the fictional residents had the intellectual wherewithal to mastermind a trip to the bathroom.

College for me was a delay fuse for the real world. As long as the fuse was burning, I didn't have to deal with the real world exploding in my face. I could hide out in Davis, attend classes to salve and pique my curiosity, write stories, go further and further into debt, work longer hours than a real job but without pay, and kid myself that this was the life.

Every Mad Dog Has His Day taps into the college spirit of the students on the fringes, not the pre-med late-night-oil-burner types. These students ducked in under the wire into liberal arts majors with no jobs waiting on the other side of the educational equation. (I graduated as one but defected to high-tech in a not entirely futile attempt to get paid for being a student. Please don't tell my former employers.) While serious students studied, these freewheelers played pranks, took barber-chair tequila shots, excelled at beer pong, and probably had not a few adventures with a certain dummy (that's ambiguous, darn it…). Fictional adventures.

If you don't buy that, the characters in the story plead youthful enthusiasm, a fifth of bourbon, and plausible deniability, combined with a travel visa, flight reservations, and a waiting Uber.

Behind the Scenes of The Great Cafeteria Food Fight and Ice Cream Raid of 1981

I wrote *The Great Cafeteria Food Fight and Ice Cream Raid of 1981* in late 2022, more than forty years after it didn't happen. After all these decades, the time had come to reveal the truth. Or something like the truth. Or something nothing like the truth and more resembling the fantasy of every student who ever ate at a cafeteria.

The characters represent the people who would have been involved in the real event had it occurred. If any of the people who were not involved read this story, they will recognize the blatant falsehoods and assassinations of their characters with righteous indignation and perhaps fond recollection.

If I've broken a pact of silence that never existed about these fictional events and that results in the people who were not involved hunting me down and killing me, as per the mutual pact we never made, I will look at it on the bright side: I hear books sell better after the author suffers a grisly and well-publicized death.

This adventure would have been impossible in today's "cameras everywhere" society, thus the story could not take place on a modern campus. Fortunately, in 1981 there were no cameras inside or outside the Dining Commons and cell phones didn't exist yet, so much like the number of licks it takes to get to the center of a Tootsie Pop, the world may never know.

Behind the Scenes of The Irate Businessman

I came up with the idea for *The Irate Businessman* and its first few scenes in the late 1990s or early 2000s when I was feeling particularly snippy about the way some television ministries (I use the term *ministries* loosely while those same ministries often use the term sacrilegiously) take advantage of honest believers and fleece people who really, really need the money. But it seems that some of these ministers (again, loose usage of the term) need diamond rings and mansions and fancy clothes even more than other people need food to eat, medical services, or basic shelter.

In spite of or perhaps because of my state of agitated snippiness, I couldn't finish the story. This sometimes happens, and when it does, I practice the time-honored strategy of masterful inactivity. Some uncouth people call that giving up, others call it sitting on your bum with your thumb up your nether region, and still others call it utter lack of imagination or *what makes you think you're a writer, eh?* However, I prefer to think of it as delayed writification.

Against all odds, in the summer of 2017, the masterful inactivity strategy paid off when Schach, Pandy, and the Archangel Gabriel entered the story, and suddenly there actually was a story. Now go pray real hard for something you really want and can actually give yourself, then give it to yourself. Remember, God helps those who help themselves. I know of a lot of corporate CEOs who really run with that idea.

Behind the Scenes of I Am

I wrote the first version of *I Am* in 1979, when I was still in high school. The story idea came after reading a statement that an editor of a popular science fiction magazine wrote. The editor said he was automatically rejecting all stories about time machines and time travel because it had all been done before, there were no new twists, and nobody could write anything new on the subject. Case closed.

My reaction was, "Oh, ye of little faith…and no sense of irony… you edit a magazine that caters to science fiction, a genre that's all about ingenuity and innovation, yet you give writers so little credit for being able to innovate ingeniously."

Of course, being a high school twit, I had to prove the editor wrong. So, in a very conventional and inexperienced way, I tried to brute force a new idea for time travel and time machines. I thought about what little I knew about physics and all the science fiction stories I'd read. Nothing. I think that effort birthed the sarcastic sitcom staple, "That went well."

That's not the way stories happen. This is one of the ways stories happen: I wasn't thinking of anything in particular, then a situation and a story-ending line just popped into my mind. At first, I didn't think of the idea in terms of time travel. It seemed more like an explanation of God. That's why I chose a biblically referential title:

"And God said unto Moses, I Am That I Am: and he said, Thus shalt thou say unto the children of Israel, I Am hath sent me unto you." (Exodus 3:7–8, 13–14).

The ending line that I dreamed up was, "So get up and pour yourself a drink, because I'm thirsty." The situation was that the speaker was simultaneously a part of everyone, everywhere, everywhen. If you drank, the narrator's thirst was slaked.

I liked the idea, so I sat down and started working out a story that would result in that situation and in that last line. This is the only story I've constructed by coming up with the last line first and then building a story to get to that ending.

As I worked on the story, time machines and time travel still lurked in the recesses of my mind. I realized I could answer the question, "How did the character become part of everyone, everywhere, everywhen?" with "a time machine." Only this wasn't your pulp fiction time machine or any other time machine cliché; this one worked much differently. It worked simultaneously across all space and across all time. As far as I know as of this writing, *I Am* presents a new take on old time machine and time travel tropes.

Although…I never did hear back from that editor.

Behind the Scenes of The Gardener

The Gardener is a recent story, written in 2024. As I prepared the story *I Am* for the book, for reasons unknown, I started thinking about the Big Bang Theory. The result was *The Gardener*. I starting writing a few notes and then the story spilled out. Or perhaps, The Aristocrats willed it from my flying fingers. This story instantiated itself whole in my mind, from The Aristocrats to The Gardener to The Seed to The End. I knew where the story was going and gave my characters free rein to get there in their own way. The story didn't turn out as alike to *I Am* as I feared it would when I was making notes at the start. It stands as its own unique story.

Although *The Gardener* and *I Am* are thematically similar, the characters are very different, the feel is very different, and the outcome is very different. The commonality is that they both are part of what I talk about when I talk about God. I also view these two short stories as bookends that show how my style and voice have changed and how they have stayed the same over a long period of time.

There's little you need to "read into" in *I Am*, it's all pretty much laid out from the mind of a teenager.

There are a few little things in *The Gardener* that aren't completely spelled out. One is that The Aristocrats' names begin with A, B, and C. The ABCs, the basics, the building blocks. Another is that The Aristocrats and the constructs they instantiate do not have pronouns, because they are composed of energy and do not have gender as we know it. The only pronouns in the story come when The Gardener finishes creating The Seed, and for the first time, The Gardener feels pride. Pride is personal. Feeling pride opens the door of self-awareness and creates the need for a personal pronoun.

Not using pronouns was a challenge. It's difficult not to use personal pronouns (no I, he, she, her, him, his, hers, etc.) while at the same time avoiding repeating "The Gardener" six times in two lines.

We may never know if The Aristocrats found enough energy to start up a little universe. Perhaps they fought, made alliances, and eventually overcame one of their group, only to find that the energy from one Aristocrat was not enough to start up a new universe. That, of course, would leave the question: is the energy of *two* Aristocrats enough to start up a little universe?

ORIGINATION

S.L. LEITNER

About the Cover Illustration and Title

I struggled with the title of this, my first published book. My original cover concept was based on a photo a friend took of a partial eclipse of the sun while we were on a road trip in Texas Hill Country in October of 2023. That inspired me to title the book *A Partial Eclipse of the Brain*. The idea was to create a cover split in half vertically. The top half would be black with the photo of the eclipse and its corona popping out of it. The black would bleed into the bottom half of the cover, which would be bright red. On that red would be an illustration of a partially eclipsed white/gray brain.

When we started to work on cover art, it turned out that the photo's resolution wasn't high enough. We tried to recreate the eclipse, but we couldn't design anything we liked or that had the power of the original photo.

I later realized that the original title and cover concept were, as a friend put it, a bit on-the-nose, as in too literal. Much too literal, in hindsight.

Fortunately, my daughter, who is a graphic designer, thought about it for a few days and came up with a different spin on the idea, the one you see on the cover today. Instead of a partial eclipse shading part of a white/gray brain, she created a full eclipse *within* a translucent brain, illuminating the translucent part of the brain while also concealing its unknowable mystery in the blackness of the eclipse.

I loved it.

Beautiful, simple, powerful. Several friends saw it and loved it too. But…solving one problem often creates another.

In this case, the problem created was that the title *A Partial Eclipse of the Brain* was no longer quite right. At that time, I hadn't yet gained enough distance from my original concept to understand that it wasn't as good I first thought it was. The thought of "killing my darling" by changing that beloved title made me shiver.

But there comes a time when one knows it's over and there's only one thing one can do. I shot *A Partial Eclipse of the Brain* right in the back of the head, gangland style, and sent it to Hades where it joined the screaming hordes of my other discarded titles, character names, and clever little stupid phrases that delight no one.

Then I thought about that beautiful illustration and visualized it in my mind. Its symbolism slowly penetrated the layers of my psyche, inspired my imagination. The impenetrable black ball of the eclipse in middle of the brain, the middle of the mind. The unknown and unknowable source, the black box of creativity and ideation from which concepts erupt in magnificent fiery streamers of uniqueness, their origins buried in the depths of the eclipsed middle of the mind. Many ask, "Where do writers get their ideas?" Here. Here. They originate in the unknown depths of the mind.

That's when I knew the new title had to be *Origination*. The black ball of the eclipse and the brilliance of its corona within the brain are the black box of creativity within the mind, the unknown and unknowable origination of unique ideas and concepts. The corona shines out from those unknown origins to illuminate the unknown and to transform it into something we can know. These are also my original stories—they originated with me. And this is my first published book, the origination of a stream of stories and novels to come. And that all seems right, so I went with the title *Origination*. What do you think?

⧖ ⧖ ⧖ ⧖ ⧖

A further thought in postscript: there's a quantum aspect at play, too. The widely accepted Hawking Radiation theory posits that through quantum interactions (entanglement), particles such as quarks, electrons, and photons can escape the event threshold of a black hole and pop into existence in normal space. What happens inside black holes is theorized, but we cannot see inside to find out what's really happening. But if the theory is correct, we can find some evidence of what's going on in the particles that escape the black hole's influence.

In the same way, the impenetrable black ball of creativity in the mind is impossible to see inside. We can't know how it works, how thoughts mesh and make connections between things that have no apparent relationship, how unique characters and unique universes spring to life. Like the Hawking Radiation particles that pop out of a black hole, story and character and universe ideas pop out from that impenetrable world of creativity in the mind into normal space—the normal space of the brain, the consciousness, where the writer can grasp them and put them to words, brought forth from their origination in the unknown depths of the mind.

S.L. LEITNER

About the Author

I knew at a relatively early age that I would become a professional writer. I can't imagine being or doing anything else. I know, I know, writers are supposed to have more imagination than that.

After college and a few odd jobs that included teaching PE at a middle school and being a tour guide in Europe, I made my living as a writer for thirty-seven years, although technically, not as a fiction writer. Technically, I was a technical writer. I wrote about cybersecurity, post-quantum cryptography, zero trust networks—you know, light reading. (Those who are familiar with the term *vaporware* understand that sometimes a lot more fiction is involved than the term *technical writer* might seem to imply.) But perhaps it's better, or longer anyway, to start at the beginning.

After shuffling from domicile to domicile and school to school as my parents bounced around the San Francisco bay area, my parents realized they were too restless for one state or even for one country and moved to Australia. We traveled across most of the country for about a year, often driving 10-12 hours a day through the Outback, before settling in Sydney, where I attended 4th grade. In the back seat of the car, I became an avid reader and started writing stories. Eventually, I submitted a story to a young writers contest and won. I still suspect that my competitors were mainly kangaroos.

Eventually, my dad decided he wanted to go back to the U.S., and, despite a three-day temper tantrum from yours truly, back we went. My writing bug went dormant until I reached junior high school and took an elective story writing class. The writing bug burst out of its cocoon and it was on. I wrote a story about 20 times the required length for the class, about a group of scientists trying to tap the Earth's core for heat to convert into energy. All the characters had the last names of Dallas Cowboys and Minnesota Vikings football players because I was an avid football fan, player, and card collector. (It was only upon entering high school that I became a 49ers lifer, even though they were terrible in the late '70s.)

By the time I entered high school, my friends had abandoned their girlish dreams of being football players, fireman, or rich executives, and instead embraced the who-gives-a-damn punk-era ennui. I, however, still had my girlish dreams. The rest of them had no idea what they wanted to do, but I wanted to be a writer and inflict stories on the unsuspecting public.

I wrote many short, amateurish stories that nonetheless impressed my peers and caused my writing teachers to encourage my development. Then either late in my junior year or early in my senior year, I finally wrote a story that I really liked, and it's in this book: *I Am*. Writing that story reinforced that I was meant to be a writer, that I was capable of coming up with unique ideas.

After high school, I decided to punt on adulthood and play defense. I went to the University of California at Davis and majored in English with a concentration in Creative Writing. That was where I had the good fortune to be chosen for a creative writing class taught by guest lecturer and Hugo and Nebula Award winning writer Kim Stanley Robinson. (How's that for name-dropping? I'll stop now, but only because I have no more names to drop.) The hidden beauty of the degree was that it took barely over a third of the units required for graduation to complete, so I had a lot of latitude to take whatever subjects piqued my interest. I took physics, biology, educational law, symbolic logic, biofeedback, German; I did a psych minor too and had units to spare for a history class.

Eventually, the university noticed that I had accumulated enough units to graduate and nudged me with a very sharp stick into graduation, but still I refused to join adulthood. I asked my family to forgo buying me a nice suit and watch, neither of which I would ever have worn, and instead buy me a plane ticket to Europe and a Eurail pass. They politely informed me they never had any intention of buying me a suit or a watch or even a new pair of socks, but in order to get rid of me, they'd buy me a one-way ticket to the cheapest airport in Europe.

On a budget of about six dollars a day derived from selling everything I had that wasn't bolted down, I spent the next three months bopping around Western Europe. I popped in on the Montreux Jazz Festival and listened to music at the free venues and from outside of the pay venues with a horde of other young venturers. I joined new friends I met on a train in Spain three weeks later for their annual town celebration weekend in Peißenberg, Germany. We watched a boxing match against another town and sang songs I didn't know but somehow did in the middle of the road at 3 a.m., still with Maßes (liter-sized glass mugs) of beer in our hands. I spent a week with my aunt and cousins in Barcelona. I saw an incredible concert with Herbie Hancock, Wayne Shorter, and Tony Williams (among others) in the ruins of a Roman coliseum in Lyon. A song from that performance is in the 1986 movie *Round Midnight*.

Eventually, I made my way back to California, and, because the rent refused to magically pay itself, I wound up teaching P.E. to middle schoolers. It was exactly as much of a blast as you're imagining and about two seconds into it (I'm a bit slow sometimes), I realized I had to make my living as a writer. A Silicon Valley survey of the obvious led to two choices: newspaper reporter or technical writer. I thank God every day that I chose technical writer. I chose technical writer because it's the closest thing to getting paid to be a student. Not paid much, but paid.

I also figured that writing every day had to be good for my fiction writing chops. *Man, was I wrong*. After staring at a screen and writing all day at work, the last thing I wanted to do was sit in front of a screen at night. I became a better and better tech writer but only wrote new stories sporadically. I still had plenty of ideas, but motivation and time were harder to come by.

A few years ago, despite being beaten down by screen fatigue, my motivation magically returned. I had been talking with a friend at work, Doug Purcell, about writing. It turned out he wrote a book called *The Art and Science of Self-Publishing* (helped me a lot), which you can buy on Amazon along with four other books Doug wrote and self-published on computer programming topics. At around the same time I was talking with

Doug, my daughter graduated. She was coming home from school with her cats to stay for an undetermined while and get her financial footing. The confluence of those two things somehow got me writing again. Even though I was still working a ten-hour Silicon Valley day five days a week and six on weekends, I was suddenly motivated to sit down late at night and write.

The only problem was that now my ten-hour Silicon Valley day was morphing into a sixteen-hour crazy person's day. Eventually, sleep deprivation led to the epiphany that I could just as easily starve without a Silicon Valley job as with one, so I quit and am now happily writing away and trying not to think about trivialities like food and rent.

The first result of kicking paying work to the curb is *Origination*, which combines my newest stories with the best of my older stories. I'm currently working on a bioscience fiction novel based on CRISPR-Cas9 gene editing technology, which I hope to complete and publish within 12-16 months of publishing *Origination*.

Thanks for reading!

— *S.L. Leitner, Santa Clara, California, September 2025.*

ORIGINATION

S.L. LEITNER

Made in the USA
Coppell, TX
08 January 2026